Overnight to Many Distant Cities

BY DONALD BARTHELME

Come Back, Dr. Caligari
Snow White
Unspeakable Practices, Unnatural Acts
City Life
Sadness
Guilty Pleasures
The Dead Father
Amateurs
Great Days
Sixty Stories
Overnight to Many Distant Cities

FOR CHILDREN

The Slightly Irregular Fire Engine

Overnight to
Many Distant Cities

Donald Barthelme

G. P. Putnam's Sons / New York

Copyright © 1983 by Donald Barthelme
All rights reserved. This book, or parts thereof,
must not be reproduced in any form without permission.
Published simultaneously in Canada by
Academic Press Canada Limited, Toronto.

Of the stories in this book, the following originally appeared in
The New Yorker, some in slightly different form: "Visitors,"
"Financially, the paper . . . ," "Affection," "Lightning," "Captain
Blood," "Conversations With Goethe," "The Sea of Hesitation,"
"When he came . . . ," "The Mothball Fleet," "Wrack," "On our
street . . . ," "The Palace at Four A.M.," and "Overnight to Many
Distant Cities." The author is grateful to *The New Yorker* for
permission to reprint.

THE TEXT OF THIS BOOK IS SET IN BASKERVILLE.

Designed by Richard Oriolo

Library of Congress Cataloging in Publication Data

Barthelme, Donald.
Overnight to many distant cities.

I. Title.
PS3552.A7609   1983   813'.54   83-4594
ISBN 0-399-12868-9

Printed in the United States of America

To Marion

Contents

They called for more structure, then, so we brought in some big hairy four-by-fours from the back shed and nailed them into place with railroad spikes. This new city, they said, was going to be just jim-dandy, would make architects stutter, would make Chambers of Commerce burst into flame. We would have our own witch doctors, and strange gods aplenty, and site-specific sins, and humuhumunukunukuapuaa in the public fish bowls. We workers listened with our mouths agape. We had never heard anything like it. But we trusted our instincts and our paychecks, so we pressed on, bringing in color-coated steel from the back shed and anodized aluminum from the shed behind that. Oh radiant city! we said to ourselves, how we want you to be built! Workplace democracy was practiced on the job, and the clerk-of-the-works (who had known Wiwi Lönn in Finland) wore a little cap with a little feather, very jaunty. There was never any question of hanging back (although we noticed that our ID cards were of a color different from their ID cards); the exercise of our skills, and the promise of the city, were enough. By the light of the moon we counted our chisels and told stories of other building feats we had been involved in: Babel, Chandigarh, Brasilia, Taliesin.

At dawn each day, an eight-mile run, to condition ourselves for the implausible exploits ahead.

The enormous pumping station, clad in red Lego, at the point where the new river will be activated . . .

Areas of the city, they told us, had been designed to rot, fall into desuetude, return, in time, to open space. Perhaps, they said, fawns would one day romp there, on the crumbling brick. We were slightly skeptical about this part of the plan, but it was, after all, a plan, the ferocious integrity of the detailing impressed us all, and standing by the pens containing the fawns who would father the fawns who might some day romp on the crumbling brick, one could not help but notice one's chest bursting with anticipatory pride.

High in the air, working on a setback faced with alternating bands of gray and rose stone capped with grids of gray glass, we moistened our brows with the tails of our shirts, which had been dipped into a pleasing brine, lit new cigars, and saw the new city spread out beneath us, in the shape of the word FASTIGIUM. Not the name of the city, they told us, simply a set of letters selected for the elegance of the script. The little girl dead behind the rosebushes came back to life, and the passionate construction continued.

Visitors

———————————————————

It's three o'clock in the morning.

Bishop's daughter is ill, stomach pains. She's sleeping on the couch.

Bishop too is ill, chills and sweating, a flu. He can't sleep. In bed, he listens to the occasional groans from two rooms away. Katie is fifteen and spends the summer with him every year.

Outside on the street, someone kicks on a motorcycle and revs it unforgivingly. His bedroom is badly placed.

He's given her Pepto-Bismol, if she wakes again he'll try Tylenol. He wraps himself in the sheet, pulls his t-shirt away from his damp chest.

There's a radio playing somewhere in the building, big-band music, he feels rather than hears it. The steady, friendly air-conditioner hustling in the next room.

Earlier he'd taken her to a doctor, who found nothing. "You've got a bellyache," the doctor said,

"stick with fluids and call me if it doesn't go away."
Katie is beautiful, tall with dark hair.

In the afternoon they'd gone, groaning, to a horror movie about wolves taking over the city. At vivid moments she jumped against him, pressing her breasts into his back. He moved away.

When they walk together on the street she takes his arm, holding on tightly (because, he figures, she spends so much of her time away, away). Very often people give them peculiar looks.

He's been picking up old ladies who've been falling down in front of him, these last few days. One sitting in the middle of an intersection waving her arms while dangerous Checkers curved around her. The old ladies invariably display a superb fighting spirit. "Thank you, young man!"

He's forty-nine. Writing a history of 19th Century American painting, about which he knows a thing or two.

Not enough.

A groan, heartfelt but muted, from the other room. She's awake.

He gets up and goes in to look at her. The red-and-white cotton robe she's wearing is tucked up under her knees. "I just threw up again," she says.

"Did it help?"

"A little."

He once asked her what something (a box? a chair?) was made of and she told him it was made out of tree.

"Do you want to try a glass of milk?"

"I don't want any milk," she says, turning to lie on her front. "Sit with me."

He sits on the edge of the couch and rubs her back. "Think of something terrific," he says. "Let's get your mind off your stomach. Think about fishing. Think about the time you threw the hotel keys out of the window." Once, in Paris, she had done just that, from a sixth-floor window, and Bishop had had visions of some Frenchman walking down the Quai des Grands-Augustins with a set of heavy iron hotel keys buried in his brain. He'd found the keys in a potted plant outside the hotel door.

"Daddy," she says, not looking at him.

"Yes?"

"Why do you live like this? By yourself?"

"Who am I going to live with?"

"You could find somebody. You're handsome for your age."

"Oh very good. That's very neat. I thank you."

"You don't try."

This is and is not true.

"How much do you weigh?"

"One eighty-five."

"You could lose some weight."

"Look, kid, gimme a break." He blots his forehead with his arm. "You want some cambric tea?"

"You've given up."

"Not so," he says. "Katie, go to sleep now. Think of a great big pile of Gucci handbags."

She sighs and turns her head away.

Bishop goes into the kitchen and turns on the light. He wonders what a drink would do to him, or for him—put him to sleep? He decides against it. He turns on the tiny kitchen TV and spends a few minutes watching some kind of Japanese monster movie. The poorly designed monster is picking up handfuls of people and, rather thoughtfully, eating them. Bishop thinks about Tokyo. He was once in bed with a Japanese girl during a mild earthquake, and he's never forgotten the feeling of the floor falling out from underneath him, or the woman's terror. He suddenly remembers her name, Michiko. "You no butterfly on me?" she had asked, when they met. He was astonished to learn that "butterfly" meant, in the patois of the time, "abandon." She cooked their meals over a charcoal brazier and they slept in a niche in the wall closed off from the rest of her room by sliding paper doors. Bishop worked on the copy desk at *Stars & Stripes*. One day a wire photo came in showing the heads of the four (then) women's services posing for a group portrait. Bishop slugged the caption LEADING LADIES. The elderly master sergeant who was serving as city editor brought the photo back to Bishop's desk. "We can't do this," he said. "Ain't it a shame?"

He switches channels and gets Dolly Parton singing, by coincidence, "House of the Rising Sun."

At some point during each summer she'll say: "Why did you and my mother split up?"

"It was your fault," he answers. "Yours. You made too much noise, as a kid, I couldn't work." His ex-wife had once told Katie this as an explanation for the divorce, and he'll repeat it until its untruth is marble, a monument.

His ex-wife is otherwise very sensible, and thrifty, too.

Why do I live this way? Best I can do.

Walking down West Broadway on a Saturday afternoon. Barking art caged in the high white galleries, don't go inside or it'll get you, leap into your lap and cover your face with kisses. Some goes to the other extreme, snarls and shows its brilliant teeth. O art I won't hurt you if you don't hurt me. Citizens parading, plump-faced and bone-faced, lightly clad. A young black boy toting a Board of Education trombone case. A fellow with oddly-cut hair the color of marigolds and a roll of roofing felt over his shoulder.

Bishop in the crowd, thirty dollars in his pocket in case he has to buy a pal a drink.

Into a gallery because it must be done. The artist's hung twenty EVERLAST heavy bags in rows of four, you're invited to have a bash. People are giving the bags every kind of trouble. Bishop, unable to resist, bangs one with his fabled left, and hurts his hand.

Bloody artists.

Out on the street again, he is bumped into by a man, then another man, then a woman. And here's Harry in lemon pants with his Britisher friend, Malcolm.

"Harry, Malcolm."

"Professor," Harry says ironically (he is a professor, Bishop is not).

Harry's got not much hair and has lost weight since he split with Tom. Malcolm is the single most cheerful individual Bishop has ever met.

Harry's university has just hired a new president who's thirty-two. Harry can't get over it.

"Thirty-two! I mean I don't think the board's got both oars in the water."

Standing behind Malcolm is a beautiful young woman.

"This is Christie," Malcolm says. "We've just given her lunch. We've just eaten all the dim sum in the world."

Bishop is immediately seized by a desire to cook for Christie—either his Eight-Bean Soup or his Crash Cassoulet.

She's telling him something about her windows.

"I don't care but why under my windows?"

She's wearing a purple shirt and is deeply tanned with black hair—looks like an Indian, in fact, the one who sells Mazola on TV.

Harry is still talking about the new president. "I mean he did his dissertation on *bathing trends.*"

"Well maybe he knows where the big bucks are."
There's some leftover duck in the refrigerator he
can use for the cassoulet.

"Well," he says to Christie, "are you hungry?"

"Yes," she says, "I am."

"We just ate," Harry says. "You can't be hungry.
You can't possibly be hungry."

"Hungry, hungry, hungry," she says, taking Bishop's arm, which is, can you believe it, sticking out.

Putting slices of duck in bean water while Christie
watches "The Adventures of Robin Hood," with Errol Flynn and Basil Rathbone, on the kitchen TV. At
the same time Hank Williams Jr. is singing on the
FM.

"I like a place where I can take my shoes off," she
says, as Errol Flynn throws a whole dead deer on the
banquet table.

Bishop, chopping parsley, is taking quick glances
at her to see what she looks like with a glass of wine
in her hand. Some people look good with white
wine, some don't.

He makes a mental note to buy some Mazola—a
case, maybe.

"Here's sixty seconds on fenders," says the radio.

"Do you live with anybody?" Christie asks.

"My daughter is here sometimes. Summers and
Christmas." A little tarragon into the bean water.
"How about you?"

"There's this guy."

But there had to be. Bishop chops steadfastly with
his Three Sheep brand Chinese chopper, made in
gray Fusan.

"He's an artist."

As who is not? "What kind of an artist?"

"A painter. He's in Seattle. He needs rain."

He throws handfuls of sliced onions into the water, then a can of tomato paste.

"How long does this take?" Christie asks. "I'm not rushing you, I'm just curious."

"Another hour."

"Then I'll have a little vodka. Straight. Ice. If you don't mind."

Bishop loves women who drink.

Maybe she smokes!

"Actually I can't stand artists," she says.

"Like who in particular?"

"Like that woman who puts chewing gum on her stomach—"

"She doesn't do that any more. And the chewing gum was not poorly placed."

"And that other one who cuts off parts of himself, *whittles* on himself, that fries my ass."

"It's supposed to."

"Yeah," she says, shaking the ice in her glass. "I'm reacting like a bozo."

She gets up and walks over to the counter and takes a Lark from his pack.

Very happily, Bishop begins to talk. He tells her that the night before he had smelled smoke, had gotten up and checked the apartment, knowing that a pier was on fire over by the river and suspecting it was that. He had turned on the TV to get the all-news channel and while dialing had encountered the opening credits of a Richard Widmark cop film called "Brock's Last Case" which he had then sat down and watched, his faithful Scotch at his side, until five o'clock in the morning. Richard Widmark was one of his favorite actors in the whole world, he told her, because of the way in which Richard Widmark was able to convey, what was the word, resilience. You could knock Richard Widmark down, he said, you could even knock Richard Widmark down repeatedly, but you had better bear in mind while knocking Richard Widmark down that Richard Widmark was pretty damn sure going to bounce back up and batter your conk—

"Redford is the one I like," she says.

Bishop can understand this. He nods seriously.

"The thing I like about Redford is," she says, and for ten minutes she tells him about Robert Redford.

He tastes the cassoulet with a long spoon. More salt.

It appears that she is also mighty fond of Clint Eastwood.

Bishop has the sense that the conversation has strayed, like a bad cow, from the proper path.

"Old Clint Eastwood," he says, shaking his head admiringly. "We're ready."

He dishes up the cassoulet and fetches hot bread from the oven.

"Tastes like real cassoulet," she says.

"That's the ox-tail soup mix." Why is he serving her cassoulet in summer? It's hot.

He's opened a bottle of Robert Mondavi table red.

"*Very* good," she says. "I mean I'm surprised. Really."

"Maybe could have had more tomato."

"No, really." She tears off a fistful of French bread. "Men are quite odd. I saw this guy at the farmer's market on Union Square on Saturday? He was standing in front of a table full of greens and radishes and corn and this and that, behind a bunch of other people, and he was staring at this farmer-girl who was wearing cut-offs and a tank top and every time she leaned over to grab a cabbage or whatnot he was getting a shot of her breasts, which were, to be fair, quite pretty—I mean how much fun can that be?"

"Moderate amount of fun. Some fun. Not much fun. What can I say?"

"And that plug I live with."

"What about him?"

"He gave me a book once."

"What was it?"

"Book about how to fix home appliances. The dishwasher was broken. Then he bought me a screwdriver. This really nice screwdriver."

"Well."

"I *fixed* the damned dishwasher. Took me two days."

"Would you like to go to bed now?"

"No," Christie says, "not yet."

Not yet! Very happily, Bishop pours more wine.

Now he's sweating, little chills at intervals. He gets a sheet from the bedroom and sits in the kitchen with the sheet draped around him, guru-style. He can hear Katie turning restlessly on the couch.

He admires the way she organizes her life—that is, the way she gets done what she wants done. A little wangling, a little nagging, a little let's-go-take-a-look and Bishop has sprung for a new pair of boots, handsome ankle-height black diablo numbers that she'll wear with black ski pants . . .

Well, he doesn't give her many presents.

Could he bear a Scotch? He thinks not.

He remembers a dream in which he dreamed that his nose was as dark and red as a Bing cherry. As would be appropriate.

"Daddy?"

Still wearing the yellow sheet, he gets up and goes into the other room.

"I can't sleep."

"I'm sorry."

"Talk to me."

Bishop sits again on the edge of the couch. How large she is!

He gives her his Art History lecture.

"Then you get *Mo*-net and *Ma*-net, that's a little tricky, *Mo*-net was the one did all the water lilies and shit, his colors were blues and greens, *Ma*-net was the one did Bareass On the Grass and shit, his colors were browns and greens. Then you get Bonnard, he did all the interiors and shit, amazing light, and then you get Van Guk, he's the one with the ear and shit, and Say-zanne, he's the one with the apples and shit, you get Kandinsky, a bad mother, all them pick-up-sticks pictures, you get my man Mondrian, he's the one with the rectangles and shit, his colors were red yellow and blue, you get Moholy-Nagy, he did all the plastic thingummies and shit, you get Mar-cel Du-champ, he's the devil in human form. . . ."

She's asleep.

Bishop goes back into the kitchen and makes himself a drink.

It's five-thirty. Faint light in the big windows.

Christie's in Seattle, and plans to stay.

Looking out of the windows in the early morning he can sometimes see the two old ladies who live in the apartment whose garden backs up to his building having breakfast by candlelight. He can never figure out whether they are terminally romantic or whether, rather, they're trying to save electricity.

*Financially, the paper is quite healthy. The paper's
timberlands, mining interests, pulp and paper operations,
book, magazine, corrugated-box, and greeting-card
divisions, film, radio, television, and cable companies, and
data-processing and satellite-communications groups are
all flourishing, with over-all return on invested capital
increasing at about eleven per cent a year. Compensation
of the three highest-paid officers and directors last year
was $399,500, $362,700, and $335,400 respectively,
exclusive of profit-sharing and pension-plan accruals.*

*But top management is discouraged and saddened, and
middle management is drinking too much. Morale in the
newsroom is fair, because of the recent raises, but the
shining brows of the copy boys, traditional emblems of
energy and hope, have begun to display odd, unattractive
lines. At every level, even down into the depths of the
pressroom, where the pressmen defiantly wear their square
dirty folded-paper caps, people want management to stop
what it is doing before it is too late.*

*The new VDT machines have hurt the paper, no doubt
about it. The people in the newsroom don't like the
machines. (A few say they like the machines but these are
the same people who like the washrooms.) When the
machines go down, as they do, not infrequently, the people
in the newsroom laugh and cheer. The executive editor has
installed one-way glass in his office door, and stands
behind it looking out over the newsroom, fretting and*

groaning. Recently the paper ran the same stock tables every day for a week. No one noticed, no one complained.

Middle management has implored top management to alter its course. Top management has responded with postdated guarantees, on a sliding scale. The Guild is off in a corner, whimpering. The pressmen are holding an unending series of birthday parties commemorating heroes of labor. Reporters file their stories as usual, but if they are certain kinds of stories they do not run. A small example: the paper did not run a Holiday Weekend Death Toll story after Labor Day this year, the first time since 1926 no Holiday Weekend Death Toll story appeared in the paper after Labor Day (and the total was, although not a record, a substantial one).

Some elements of the staff are not depressed. The paper's very creative real-estate editor has been a fountain of ideas, and his sections, full of color pictures of desirable living arrangements, are choked with advertising and make the Sunday paper fat, fat, fat, fat. More food writers have been hired, and more clothes writers, and more furniture writers, and more plant writers. The bridge, whist, skat, cribbage, domino, and vingt-et-un *columnists are very popular.*

The Editors' Caucus has once again applied to middle management for relief, and has once again been promised it (but middle management has Glenfiddich on its breath, even at breakfast). Top management's polls say that sixty-five per cent of the readers "want movies," and feasibility studies are being conducted. Top management acknowledges, over long lunches at good restaurants, that the readers are wrong to "want movies" but insists that morality cannot be legislated. The newsroom has been insulated (with products from the company's Echotex division) so that the people in the newsroom can no longer hear the sounds in the streets.

The paper's editorials have been subcontracted to Texas Instruments, and the obituaries to Nabisco, so that the staff will have "more time to think." The foreign desk is turning out language lessons ("Yo temo que Isabel no venga," "I am afraid that Isabel will not come"). There was an especially lively front page on Tuesday. The No. 1 story was pepperoni—a useful and exhaustive guide. It ran right next to the slimming-your-troublesome-thighs story, with pictures.

Top management has vowed to stop what it is doing— not now but soon, soon. A chamber orchestra has been formed among the people in the newsroom, and we play Haydn until the sun comes up.

Affection

How do you want to cook this fish? How do you want to cook this fish? Harris asked.

What?

Claire heard: How do you want to cook this fish?

Breaded, she said.

Fine, Harris said.

What?

Fine!

We have not slept together for three hundred nights, she thought. We have not slept together for three hundred nights.

His rough, tender hands not wrapped around me.

Lawnmower. His rough, tender hands wrapped around the handles of the lawnmower. Not around me.

What?

Where did you hide the bread crumbs?

What?

The bread crumbs!

Behind the Cheerios!

Claire telephoned her mother. Her mother's counsel was broccoli, mostly, but who else was she going to talk to?

What?

You have to be optimistic. Be be be. Optimistic.

What?

Optimistic, her mother said, they go through phases. As they get older. They have less tolerance for monotony.

I'm monotony?

They go through phases. As they grow older. They like to think that their futures are ahead of them. This is ludicrous, of course—

Oh oh oh oh.

Ludicrous, of course, but I have never yet met one who didn't think that way until he got played out then they sink into a comfortable lassitude take to wearing those horrible old-geezer hats . . .

What?

Hats with the green plastic bills, golf hats or whatever they are—

Harris, Claire said to her husband, you've stopped watering the plants.

What?

You've stopped watering the plants my mother always said that when they stopped watering the plants that was a sure sign of an impending marital breakup.

Your mother reads too much.

What?

Sarah decided that she and Harris should not sleep together any longer.

Harris said, What about hugging?

What?

Hugging.

Sarah said that she would have a ruling on hugging in a few days and that he should stand by for further information. She pulled the black lace mantilla down to veil her face as they left the empty church.

I have done the right thing the right thing. I am right.

Claire came in wearing her brown coat and carrying a large brown paper bag. Look what I got! she said excitedly.

What? Harris said.

She reached into the bag and pulled out a smeary plastic tray with six frozen shell steaks on it. The steaks looked like they had died in the nineteenth century.

Six dollars! Claire said. This guy came into the laundromat and said he was making deliveries to restaurants and some of the restaurants already had all the steaks they needed and now he had these left over and they were only six dollars. Six dollars.

You spent six dollars on *these?*

Other people bought some too.

Diseased, stolen steaks?

He was wearing a white coat, Claire said. He had a truck.

I'll bet he had a truck.

Harris went to see Madam Olympia, a reader and advisor. Her office was one room in a bad part of the city. Chicken wings burned in a frying pan on the stove. She got up and turned them off, then got up and turned them on again. She was wearing a t-shirt that had "Buffalo, City of No Illusions" printed on it.

Tell me about yourself, she said.

My life is hell, Harris said. He sketched the circumstances.

I am bored to tears with this sort of thing, Madam Olympia said. To tears to tears.

Well, Harris said, me too.

Woman wakes up in the middle of the night, Madam Olympia said, she goes, what you thinkin' about? You go, the float. She goes, is the float makin' us money or not makin' us money? You go, it depends on what happens Wednesday. She goes, that's nice. You go, what do you mean, you don't understand *dick* about the float, woman. She goes, well you don't have to be nasty. You go, I'm *not* being nasty, you just don't *understand*. She goes, so why don't you tell me? Behind this, other agendas on both sides.

The float is a *secret*, Harris said. Many *men* don't even know about the float.

To tears to tears to tears.

Right, Harris said. How much do I owe you?

Fifty dollars.

The community whispered: Are they still living? How many times a week? What is that symbol on your breast? Did they consent to sign it? Did they refuse to sign it? In the rain? Before the fire? Has there been weight loss? How many pounds? What is their favorite color? Have they been audited? Was there a his side of the bed and a her side of the bed? Did she make it herself? Can we have a taste? Have they stolen money? Have they stolen stamps? Can he ride a horse? Can he ride a steer? What is his best time in the calf scramble? Is there money? Was there money? What happened to the money? What will happen to the money? Did success come early or late? Did success come? A red wig? At the Junior League? A red dress with a red wig? Was she ever a Fauve? Is that a theoretical position or a real position? Would they do it again? Again and again? How many times? A thousand times?

Claire met Sweet Papa Cream Puff, a new person. He was the house pianist at Bells, a club frequented by disconsolate women in the early afternoons.

He was a huge man and said that he was a living legend.

What?

Living legend, he said.

I didn't name the "Sweet Papa Cream Puff Blues" by that name, he said. It was named by the people of Chicago.

Oh my oh my oh my, Claire said.

This musta been 'bout nineteen twenty-one, twenty-two, he said.

Those was wonderful days.

There was one other man, at that time, who had part of my fame.

Fellow named Red Top, he's dead now.

He was very good, scared me a little bit.

I studied him.

I had two or three situations on the problem.

I worked very hard and bested him in nineteen twenty-three. June of that year.

Wow, Claire said.

Zum, Sweet Papa Cream Puff sang, zum zum zum zum *zum.*

Six perfect treble notes in the side pocket.

Sarah calls Harris from the clinic in Detroit and floors him with the news of her "miscarriage." Saddened by the loss of the baby, he's nevertheless elated to be free of his "obligation." But when Harris rushes to declare his love for Claire, he's crushed to learn that she is married to Sarah. Hoping against hope that Harris will stay with her, Sarah returns. Harris is hung over from drinking too much the night before when Sarah demands to know if he wants her. Unable to decide at first, he yields to Sarah's feigned helplessness and tells her to stay. Later, they share a pleasant dinner at the Riverboat, where Claire is a waiter. Harris is impressed to learn that Sarah refused to join in his mother's plan to dissuade him from becoming a policeman. Claire is embracing Harris before his departure when Sarah enters the office. When Harris is caught shoplifting, Claire's kid sister, terrified at having to face a court appearance, signs for his release. Missing Sarah terribly, Harris calls her from New Orleans; when she tells him about becoming chairwoman of Claire's new bank, he hangs up angrily. Although they've separated, his feelings for Claire haven't died entirely, and her growing involvement with his new partner, Sarah, is a bitter pill for him to swallow, as he sits alone drinking too much brandy in Sarah's study. Sarah blazes with anger when she finds Claire in the hotel's banquet office making arrangements for Harris's testimonial dinner, as Sarah, her right leg in a cast, walks up the steps of the brownstone and punches Claire's bell, rage clearly burning in her eyes.

Sarah visited Dr. Whorf, a good psychiatrist.
Cold as *death,* she said.
What?
Cold as *death.*
Good behavior is frequently painful, Dr. Whorf said. Shit you know that.

Sarah was surprised to find that what she had told Dr. Whorf was absolutely true. She was fully miserable.

Harris drunk again and yelling at Claire said that he was not drunk.

I feel worse than you feel, she said.

What?

Worse, she said, woooooooorrrssse.

You know what I saw this morning? he asked. Eight o'clock in the morning. I was out walking.

Guy comes out of this house, wearing a suit, carrying an attaché case.

He's going to work, right?

He gets about ten steps down the sidewalk and this woman comes out. Out of the same house.

She says, "James?"

He turns around and walks back toward her.

She's wearing a robe. Pink and orange.

She says, "James, *I . . . hate . . . you.*"

Maybe it's everywhere, Claire said. A pandemic.

I don't think that, Harris said.

This is the filthiest phone booth I've ever been in, Harris said to Sarah.

What?

The *filthiest phone booth* I have ever been in.

Hang up darling hang up and find another phone booth thank you for the jewels the pearls and the emeralds and the onyx but I haven't changed my mind they're quite quite beautiful just amazing but I haven't changed my mind you're so kind but I have done the right thing painful as it was and I haven't changed my mind—

He remembered her standing over the toothpaste with her face two inches from the toothpaste because she couldn't see it without her contacts in.

Freud said, Claire said, that in the adult, novelty always constitutes the condition for orgasm.

Sweet Papa looked away.

Oh me oh my.

Well you know the gents they don't know what they after they own selves, very often.

When do they find out?

At the eleventh hour let me play you a little thing I wrote in the early part of the century I call it "Verklärte Nacht" that means "stormy weather" in German, I played there in Berlin oh about—

Claire placed her arms around Sweet Papa Cream Puff and hugged the stuffing out of him.

What?

What?

What?

What?

By a lucky stroke Harris made an amount of money in the market. He bought Claire a beautiful black opal. She was pleased.

He looked to the future.

Claire will continue to be wonderful.

As will I, to the best of my ability.

The New York Times will be published every day and I will have to wash it off my hands when I have finished reading it, every day.

What? Claire said.

Smile.

What?

Smile.

I put a name in an envelope, and sealed the envelope; and put that envelope in another envelope with a spittlebug and some quantity of boric acid; and put that envelope in a still larger envelope which contained also a woman tearing her gloves to tatters; and put that envelope in the mail to Fichtelgebirge. At the Fichtelgebirge Post Office I asked if there was mail for me, with a mysterious smile the clerk said, "Yes," I hurried with the envelope to London, arriving with snow, and put the envelope in the Victoria and Albert Museum, bowing to the curators in the Envelope Room, where the wallpaper hung down in thick strips. I put the Victoria and Albert Museum in a still larger envelope which I placed in the program of the Royal Danish Ballet, in the form of an advertisement for museums, boric acid, wallpaper. I put the program of the Royal Danish Ballet into the North Sea for two weeks. Then, I retrieved it, it was hanging down in thick strips, I sent it to a machine-vask on H. C. Andersen Boulevard, everything came out square and neat, I was overjoyed. I put the square, neat package in a safe place, and put the safe place in a vault designed by Caspar David Friedrich, German romantic landscape painter of the last century. I slipped the vault into a history of art (Insel Verlag, Frankfurt, 1980). But, in a convent library on the side of a hill near a principal city of Montana, it fell out of the history of art into a wastebasket, a thing I could not have predicted. I bound the wastebasket in stone, with a matchwood shroud covering the stone, and placed it in the care of Charles the Good, Charles the Bold, and Charles the Fair. They stand juggling cork balls before the many-times-encased envelope, whispering names which are not the right one. I put the three kings into a new blue suit, it walked away from me most confidently.

Lightning

Edward Connors, on assignment for *Folks,* set out to interview nine people who had been struck by lightning. "Nine?" he said to his editor, Penfield. "Nine, ten," said Penfield, "doesn't matter, but it has to be more than eight." "Why?" asked Connors, and Penfield said that the layout was scheduled for five pages and they wanted at least two people who had been struck by lightning per page plus somebody pretty sensational for the opening page. "Slightly wonderful," said Penfield, "nice body, I don't have to tell you, somebody with a special face. Also, struck by lightning."

Connors advertised in the *Village Voice* for people who had been struck by lightning and would be willing to talk for publication about the experience and in no time at all was getting phone calls. A number of the callers, it appeared, had great-grandfathers or grandmothers who had also been struck by lightning, usually knocked from the front seat of a buckboard on a country road in 1910. Connors took down names and addresses and made appointments for interviews, trying to discern from the voices if any of the women callers might be, in the magazine's terms, wonderful.

Connors had been a reporter for ten years and a freelancer for five, with six years in between as a PR man for Topsy Oil in Midland-Odessa. As a reporter he had been excited, solid, underpaid, in love with his work, a specialist in business news, a scholar of the regulatory agencies and their eternal gavotte with the Seven Sisters, a man who knew what should be done with natural gas, with nuclear power, who knew crown blocks and monkey boards and Austin chalk, who kept his own personal hard hat ("Welltech") on top of a filing cabinet in his office. When his wife pointed out, eventually, that he wasn't making enough money (absolutely true!) he had gone with Topsy, whose PR chief had been dropping handkerchiefs in his vicinity for several years. Signing on with Topsy, he had tripled his salary, bought four moderately expensive suits, enjoyed (briefly) the esteem of his wife, and spent his time writing either incredibly dreary releases about corporate doings or speeches in praise of free enterprise for the company's C.E.O., E. H. ("Bug") Ludwig, a round, amiable, commanding man of whom he was very fond. When Connors' wife left him for a racquetball pro attached to the Big Spring Country Club he decided he could afford to be poor again and departed Topsy, renting a dismal rear apartment on Lafayette Street in New York and patching an income together by writing for a wide variety of publications, classical record reviews for *High Fidelity*, *Times* Travel pieces ("Portugal's Fabulous Beaches"), exposés for *Penthouse* ("Inside the Trilateral Commission"). To each assignment he brought a good brain, a good eye, a tenacious thoroughness, gusto. He was forty-five, making a thin living, curious about people who had been struck by lightning.

The first man he interviewed was a thirty-eight-year-old tile setter named Burch who had been struck by lightning in February 1978 and had immediately become a Jehovah's Witness. "It was the best thing that ever happened to me," said Burch, "in a way." He was a calm, rather handsome man with pale blond hair cut short, military style, and an elegantly spare (deep grays and browns) apartment in the West Twenties which looked, to Connors, as if a decorator had been involved. "I was coming back from a job in New Rochelle," said Burch, "and I had a flat. It was clouding up pretty good and I wanted to get the tire changed before the rain started. I had the tire off and was just about to put the spare on when there was this just terrific crash and I was flat on my back in the middle of the road. Knocked the tire tool 'bout a hundred feet, I found it later in a field. Guy in a VW van pulled up right in front of me, jumped out and told me I'd been struck. I couldn't hear what he was saying, I was deafened, but he made signs. Took me to a hospital and they checked me over, they were amazed—no burns, nothing, just the deafness, which lasted about forty-eight hours. I figured I owed the Lord something, and I became a Witness. And let me tell you my life since that day has been—" He paused, searching for the right word. "*Serene.* Truly serene." Burch had had a great-grandfather who had also been struck by lightning, knocked from the front seat of a buckboard on a country road in Pennsylvania in 1910, but no conversion had resulted in that case, as far as he knew. Connors arranged to have a *Folks* photographer shoot Burch on the following Wednesday and, much impressed—rarely had he encountered serenity on this scale—left the apartment with his pockets full of Witness literature.

Connors next talked to a woman named Mac-Gregor who had been struck by lightning while sitting on a bench on the Cold Spring, New York, railroad platform and had suffered third-degree burns on her arms and legs—she had been wearing a rubberized raincoat which had, she felt, protected her somewhat, but maybe not, she couldn't be sure. Her experience, while lacking a religious dimension per se, had made her think very hard about her life, she said, and there had been some important changes (*Lightning changes things,* Connors wrote in his notebook). She had married the man she had been seeing for two years but had been slightly dubious about, and on the whole, this had been the right thing to do. She and Marty had a house in Garrison, New York, where Marty was in real estate, and she'd quit her job with Estée Lauder because the commute, which she'd been making since 1975, was just too tiring. Connors made a date for the photographer. Mrs. MacGregor was pleasant and attractive (fawn-colored suit, black clocked stockings) but, Connors thought, too old to start the layout with.

The next day he got a call from someone who sounded young. Her name was Edwina Rawson, she said, and she had been struck by lightning on New Year's Day 1980 while walking in the woods with her husband, Marty. (*Two Martys in the same piece?* thought Connors, scowling.) Curiously enough, she said, her great-grandmother had also been struck by lightning, knocked from the front seat of a buggy on a country road outside Iowa City in 1911. "But I don't want to be in the magazine," she said. "I mean, with all those rock stars and movie stars. Olivia Newton-John I'm not. If you were writing a book or something—"

Connors was fascinated. He had never come across anyone who did not want to appear in *Folks* before. He was also slightly irritated. He had seen perfectly decent colleagues turn amazingly ugly when refused a request for an interview. "Well," he said, "could we at least talk? I promise I won't take up much of your time, and, you know, this is a pretty important experience, being struck by lightning— not many people have had it. Also you might be interested in how the others felt . . ." "Okay," she said, "but off the record unless I decide otherwise." "Done," said Connors. *My God, she thinks she's the State Department.*

Edwina was not only slightly wonderful but also mildly superb, worth a double-page spread in any-body's book, *Vogue, Life, Elle, Ms., Town & Country,* you name it. Oh Lord, thought Connors, there are ways and ways to be struck by lightning. She was wearing jeans and a parka and she was beautifully, beautifully black—a considerable plus, Connors noted automatically, the magazine conscientiously tried to avoid lily-white stories. She was carrying a copy of *Variety* (not an actress, he thought, *please* not an actress) and was not an actress but doing a paper on *Variety* for a class in media studies at NYU. "God, I love *Variety*," she said. "The stately march of the grosses through the middle pages." Connors de-cided that "Shall we get married?" was an inap-propriate second remark to make to one newly met, but it was a very tough decision.

They were in a bar called Bradley's on University Place in the Village, a bar Connors sometimes used for interviews because of its warmth, geniality. Ed-wina was drinking a Beck's and Connors, struck by lightning, had a feeble paw wrapped around a vodka-tonic. Relax, he told himself, go slow, we have half the afternoon. There was a kid, she said, two-

year-old boy, Marty's, Marty had split for California
and a job as a systems analyst with Warner Com-
munications, good riddance to bad rubbish. Connors had no idea what a systems analyst did: go with
the flow? The trouble with Marty, she said, was that
he was immature, a systems analyst, and white. She
conceded that when the lightning hit he had given
her mouth-to-mouth resuscitation, perhaps saved
her life; he had taken a course in CPR at the New
School, which was entirely consistent with his cau-
tious, be-prepared, white-folks' attitude toward life.
She had nothing against white folks, Edwina said
with a warm smile, or rabbits, as black folks sometimes termed them, but you had to admit that, qua
folks, they sucked. Look at the Trilateral Commission, she said, a perfect example. Connors weighed
in with some knowledgeable words about the Commission, detritus from his *Penthouse* piece, managing
to hold her interest through a second Beck's.

"Did it change your life, being struck?" asked Connors. She frowned, considered. "Yes and no," she
said. "Got rid of Marty, that was an up. Why I married him I'll never know. Why he married *me* I'll
never know. A minute of bravery, never to be repeated." Connors saw that she was much aware of
her own beauty, her hauteur about appearing in the
magazine was appropriate—who needed it? People
would dig slant wells for this woman, go out into a
producing field with a tank truck in the dead of
night and take off two thousand gallons of somebody else's crude, write fanciful checks, establish
Pyramid Clubs with tony marble-and-gold head-
quarters on Zurich's Bahnhofstrasse. What did he
have to offer?

"Can you tell me a little bit more about how you
felt when it actually hit you?" he asked, trying to
keep his mind on business. "Yes," Edwina said. "We

were taking a walk—we were at his mother's place in Connecticut, near Madison—and Marty was talking about whether or not he should take a SmokeEnders course at the Y, he smoked Kents, miles and miles of Kents. I was saying, yes, yes, do it! and whammo! the lightning. When I came to, I felt like I was burning inside, inside my chest, drank seventeen glasses of water, chug-a-lugged them, thought I was going to bust. Also, my eyebrows were gone. I looked at myself in the mirror and I had zip eyebrows. Looked really funny, maybe improved me." Regarding her closely Connors saw that her eyebrows were in fact dark dramatic slashes of eyebrow pencil. "Ever been a model?" he asked, suddenly inspired. "That's how I make it," Edwina said, "that's how I keep little Zachary in britches, look in the *Sunday Times Magazine*, I do Altman's, Macy's, you'll see me and three white chicks, usually, lingerie ads. . . ."

The soul burns, Connors thought, having been struck by lightning. Without music, Nietzsche said, the world would be a mistake. Do I have that right? Connors, no musician (although a scholar of fiddle music from Pinchas Zuckerman to Eddie South, "dark angel of the violin," 1904–1962), agreed wholeheartedly. Lightning an attempt at music on the part of God? Does get your attention, Connors thought, *attempt* wrong by definition because God is perfect by definition. . . . Lightning at once a *coup de théâtre* and career counseling? Connors wondered if he had a song to sing, one that would signify to the burned beautiful creature before him.

"The armadillo is the only animal other than man known to contract leprosy," Connors said. "The slow, friendly armadillo. I picture a leper armadillo, white as snow, with a little bell around its neck, making its draggy scamper across Texas from El Paso to Big Spring. My heart breaks."

Edwina peered into his chest where the cracked heart bumped around in its cage of bone. "Man, you are one sentimental taxpayer."

Connors signaled the waiter for more drinks. "It was about 1880 that the saintly armadillo crossed the Rio Grande and entered Texas," he said, "seeking to carry its message to that great state. Its message was, squash me on your highways. Make my nine-banded shell into beautiful lacquered baskets for your patios, decks and mobile homes. Watch me hayfoot-strawfoot across your vast savannas enriching same with my best-quality excreta. In some parts of South America armadillos grow to almost five feet in length and are allowed to teach at the junior-college level. In Argentina—"

"You're crazy, baby," Edwina said, patting him on the arm.

"Yes," Connors said, "would you like to go to a movie?"

The movie was "Moscow Does Not Believe in Tears," a nifty item. Connors, Edwina inhabiting both the right and left sides of his brain, next interviewed a man named Stupple who had been struck by lightning in April 1970 and had in consequence joined the American Nazi Party, specifically the Horst Wessel Post #66 in Newark, which had (counting Stupple) three members. *Can't use him,* thought Connors, *wasting time,* nevertheless faithfully inscribing in his notebook pages of viciousness having to do with the Protocols of Zion and the alleged genetic inferiority of blacks. *Marvelous, don't these guys ever come up with anything new?* Connors remembered having heard the same routine, almost word for word, from an Assistant Grand Dragon of the Shreveport (La.) Klan, a man somewhat dumber than a bathtub, in 1957 at the Dew Drop Inn in Shreveport, where the ribs in red sauce were not bad. Stupple, who had put on a Nazi armband over his checked flannel shirt for the interview, which was conducted in a two-room apartment over a failing four-lane bowling alley in Newark, served Connors Danish aquavit frozen into a block of ice with a very good Japanese beer, Kirin, as a chaser. "Won't you need a picture?" Stupple asked at length, and Connors said, evasively, "Well, you know, lots of people have been struck by lightning . . ."

Telephoning Edwina from a phone booth outside the Port Authority Terminal, he learned that she was not available for dinner. "How do you feel?" he asked her, aware that the question was imprecise—he really wanted to know whether having been struck by lightning was an ongoing state or, rather, a one-time illumination—and vexed by his inability to get a handle on the story. "Tired," she said, "Zach's been yelling a lot, call me tomorrow, maybe we can do something . . ."

Penfield, the *Folks* editor, had a call on Connors' service when he got back to Lafayette Street. "How's it coming?" Penfield asked. "I don't understand it yet," Connors said, "how it works. It changes people." "What's to understand?" said Penfield, "wham-bam-thank you ma'am, you got anybody I can use for the opening? We've got these terrific shots of individual bolts, I see a four-way bleed with the text reversed out of this saturated purple sky and this tiny but absolutely wonderful face looking up at the bolt—" "She's black," said Connors, "you're going to have trouble with the purple, not enough contrast." "So it'll be subtle," said Penfield excitedly, "rich and subtle. The bolt will give it enough snap. It'll be nice."

Nice, thought Connors, what a word for being struck by lightning.

Connors, trying to get at the core of the experience—did being struck exalt or exacerbate pre-existing tendencies, states of mind, and what was the relevance of electro-shock therapy, if it was a therapy?—talked to a Trappist monk who had been struck by lightning in 1975 while working in the fields at the order's Piffard, New York, abbey. Having been given permission by his superior to speak to Connors, the small, bald monk was positively loquacious. He told Connors that the one deprivation he had felt keenly, as a member of a monastic order, was the absence of rock music. "Why?" he asked rhetorically. "I'm too old for this music, it's for kids, I know it, you know it, makes no sense at all. But I love it, I simply love it. And after I was struck the community bought me this Sony Walkman." Proudly he showed Connors the small device with its delicate earphones. "A special dispensation. I guess they figured I was near-to-dead, therefore it was all right to bend the Rule a bit. I simply love it. Have you heard the Cars?" Standing in a beet field with the brown-habited monk Connors felt the depth of the man's happiness and wondered if he himself ought to re-think his attitude toward Christianity. It would not be so bad to spend one's days pulling beets in the warm sun while listening to the Cars and then retire to one's cell at night to read St. Augustine and catch up on Rod Stewart and the B-52's.

"The thing is," Connors said to Edwina that night at dinner, "I don't understand precisely what effects the change. Is it pure fright? Gratitude at having survived?" They were sitting in an Italian restaurant called Da Silvano on Sixth near Houston, eating tortellini in a white sauce. Little Zachary, a good-looking two-year-old, sat in a high chair and accepted bits of cut-up pasta. Edwina had had a shoot that afternoon and was not in a good mood. "The same damn thing," she said, "me and three white chicks,

you'd think somebody'd turn it around just once."
She needed a *Vogue* cover and a fragrance cam-
paign, she said, and then she would be sitting pretty.
She had been considered for *Hashish* some time back
but didn't get it and there was a question in her mind
as to whether her agency (Jerry Francisco) had been
solidly behind her. "Come along," said Edwina, "I
want to give you a back rub, you look a tiny bit
peaked."

Connors subsequently interviewed five more people who had been struck by lightning, uncovering
some unusual cases, including a fellow dumb from
birth who, upon being struck, began speaking quite
admirable French; his great-grandfather, as it happened, had also been struck by lightning, blasted
from the seat of a farm wagon in Brittany in 1909.
In his piece Connors described the experience as
"ineffable," using a word he had loathed and de-
spised his whole life long, spoke of lightning-as-
grace and went so far as to mention the descent of
the Dove. Penfield, without a moment's hesitation,
cut the whole paragraph, saying (correctly) that the
Folks reader didn't like "funny stuff" and pointing
out that the story was running long anyway because
of the extra page given to Edwina's opening layout,
in which she wore a Mary McFadden pleated tube
and looked, in Penfield's phrase, approximately fan-
tastic.

That guy in the back room, she said. He's eating our potatoes. You were wonderful last night. The night before that, you were wonderful. The night before that, you were terrible. He's eating our potatoes. I went in there and looked at him and he had potato smeared all over his face. Mashed. You were wonderful on the night that we met. I was terrible. You were terrible on the night we had the suckling pig. The pig, cooking the pig, put you in a terrible mood. I was wonderful in order to balance, to attempt to balance, your foul behavior. That guy with the eye patch in the back room is eating our potatoes. What are you going to do about it?

What? he said.

What are you going to do about it?

He's got a potato masher in there?

And a little pot. He holds the little pot between his knees. Mashes away with his masher. Mash mash mash.

Well, he said, he's got to live, don't he?

I don't know. Maybe so, maybe not. You brought him home. What are you going to do about it?

We have plenty of potatoes, he said. I think you're getting excited. Getting excited about nothing. Maybe you'd better simmer down. If I want frenzy I'll go out on the street. In here, I want calm. Clear, quiet calm. You're getting excited. I want you to calm down. So I can read. Quietly, read.

You were superb on the night we had the osso buco, she said. I cooked it. That seemed to strike your fancy. You appreciated the effort, my effort, or seemed to. You didn't laugh. You did smile. Smiled furiously all through dinner. I was atrocious that night. Biting the pillow. You kept the lights turned up, you were reading. We struggled for the rheostat. The music from the other room flattered you, your music, music you had bought and paid for, to flatter yourself. Your good taste. Nobody ever listens to that stuff unless he or she wants to establish that he or she has supremely good taste. Supernal good taste.

Did you know, he said, looking up, that the mayor has only one foot? One real foot?

Cooking the pig put you in a terrible mood. The pig's head in particular. You asked me to remove the pig's head. With a saw. I said that the pig's head had to remain in place. Placing the apple in a bloody hole where the pig's neck had been would be awful, I said. People would be revolted. You threw the saw on the floor and declared that you could not go on. I said that people had been putting the apple in the pig's mouth for centuries, centuries. There were twenty people coming for dinner, a mistake, of course, but not mine. The pig was stretched out on the counter. You placed the pig on two kitchen chairs which had been covered with newspaper, the floor had been covered with newspaper too, my knee was on or in the pig's back, I grasped an ear and began to saw. You were terrible that night, threw a glass of wine in a man's face. I remember these things.

Kinda funny to have a mayor with only one foot.

The man said he was going to thump you. I said, Go ahead and thump him. You said, No one is going to thump anybody. The man left, then, red wine stains staining his pink cashmere sweater quite wonderfully. You were wonderful that night.

They say, he said, that there are flowers all over the city because the mayor does not know where his mother is buried. Did you know that?

Captain Blood

When Captain Blood goes to sea, he locks the doors and windows of his house on Cow Island personally. One never knows what sort of person might chance by, while one is away.

When Captain Blood, at sea, paces the deck, he usually paces the foredeck rather than the after-deck—a matter of personal preference. He keeps marmalade and a spider monkey in his cabin, and four perukes on stands.

When Captain Blood, at sea, discovers that he is pursued by the Dutch Admiral Van Tromp, he considers throwing the women overboard. So that they will drift, like so many giant lotuses in their green, lavender, purple and blue gowns, across Van Tromp's path, and he will have to stop and pick them up. Blood will have the women fitted with life jackets under their dresses. They will hardly be in much danger at all. But what about the jaws of sea turtles? No, the women cannot be thrown overboard. Vile, vile! What an idiotic idea! What could he have been thinking of? Of the patterns they would have made floating on the surface of the water, in the moonlight, a cerise gown, a silver gown . . .

Captain Blood presents a façade of steely imperturbability.

He is poring over his charts, promising everyone that things will get better. There has not been one bit of booty in the last eight months. Should he try another course? Another ocean? The men have been quite decent about the situation. Nothing has been said. Still, it's nerve-racking.

When Captain Blood retires for the night (leaving orders that he be called instantly if something comes up) he reads, usually. Or smokes, thinking calmly of last things.

His hideous reputation should not, strictly speaking, be painted in the horrible colors customarily employed. Many a man walks the streets of Panama City, or Port Royal, or San Lorenzo, alive and well, who would have been stuck through the gizzard with a rapier, or smashed in the brain with a boarding pike, had it not been for Blood's swift, cheerful intervention. Of course, there are times when severe measures are unavoidable. At these times he does not flinch, but takes appropriate action with admirable steadiness. There are no two ways about it: when one looses a seventy-four-gun broadside against the fragile hull of another vessel, one gets carnage.

Blood at dawn, a solitary figure pacing the foredeck.

No other sail in sight. He reaches into the pocket of his blue velvet jacket trimmed with silver lace. His hand closes over three round, white objects: mothballs. In disgust, he throws them over the side. One *makes* one's luck, he thinks. Reaching into another pocket, he withdraws a folded parchment tied with ribbon. Unwrapping the little packet, he finds that it is a memo that he wrote to himself ten months earlier. *"Dolphin,* Captain Darbraunce, 120 tons, cargo silver, paprika, bananas, sailing Mar. 10 Havana. *Be there!"* Chuckling, Blood goes off to seek his mate, Oglethorpe—that laughing blond giant of a man.

Who will be aboard this vessel which is now within cannon-shot? wonders Captain Blood. Rich people, I hope, with pretty gold and silver things aplenty.

"Short John, where is Mr. Oglethorpe?"

"I am not Short John, sir. I am John-of-Orkney."

"Sorry, John. Has Mr. Oglethorpe carried out my instructions?"

"Yes, sir. He is forward, crouching over the bombard, lit cheroot in hand, ready to fire."

"Well, fire then."

"Fire!"

BAM!

"The other captain doesn't understand what is happening to him!"

"He's not heaving to!"

"He's ignoring us!"

"The dolt!"

"Fire again!"

BAM!

"That did it!"

"He's turning into the wind!"

"He's dropped anchor!"

"He's lowering sail!"

"Very well, Mr. Oglethorpe. You may prepare to board."

"Very well, Peter."

"And Jeremy—"

"Yes, Peter?"

"I know we've had rather a thin time of it these last few months."

"Well it hasn't been so bad, Peter. A little slow, perhaps—"

"Well, before we board, I'd like you to convey to the men my appreciation for their patience. Patience and, I may say, tact."

"We knew you'd turn up something, Peter."

"Just tell them for me, will you?"

Always a wonderful moment, thinks Captain Blood. Preparing to board. Pistol in one hand, naked cutlass in the other. Dropping lightly to the deck of the engrappled vessel, backed by one's grinning, leering, disorderly, rapacious crew who are nevertheless under the strictest buccaneer discipline. There to confront the little band of fear-crazed victims shrinking from the entirely possible carnage. Among them, several beautiful women, but one really spectacular beautiful woman who stands a bit apart from her sisters, clutching a machete with which she intends, against all reason, to—

When Captain Blood celebrates the acquisition of a rich prize, he goes down to the galley himself and cooks *tallarínes a la Catalana* (noodles, spare ribs, almonds, pine nuts) for all hands. The name of the captured vessel is entered in a little book along with the names of all the others he has captured in a long career. Here are some of them: the *Oxford*, the *Luis*, the *Fortune*, the *Lambe*, the *Jamaica Merchant*, the *Betty*, the *Prosperous*, the *Endeavor*, the *Falcon*, the *Bonadventure*, the *Constant Thomas*, the *Marquesa*, the *Señora del Carmen*, the *Recovery*, the *Maria Gloriosa*, the *Virgin Queen*, the *Esmerelda*, the *Havana*, the *San Felipe*, the *Steadfast* . . .

The true buccaneer is not persuaded that God is not on his side, too—especially if, as is often the case, he turned pirate after some monstrously unjust thing was done to him, such as being press-ganged into one or another of the Royal Navies when he was merely innocently having a drink at a waterfront tavern, or having been confined to the stinking dungeons of the Inquisition just for making some idle, thoughtless, light remark. Therefore, Blood feels himself to be devout *in his own way,* and has endowed candles burning in churches in most of the great cities of the New World. Although not under his own name.

Captain Blood roams ceaselessly, making daring raids. The average raid yields something like 20,000 pieces-of-eight, which is apportioned fairly among the crew, with wounded men getting more according to the gravity of their wounds. A cut ear is worth two pieces, a cut-*off* ear worth ten to twelve. The scale of payments for injuries is posted in the forecastle.

When he is on land, Blood is confused and troubled by the life of cities, where every passing stranger may, for no reason, assault him, if the stranger so chooses. And indeed, the stranger's mere presence, multiplied many times over, is a kind of assault. Merely having to *take into account* all these hurrying others is a blistering occupation. This does not happen on a ship, or on a sea.

An amusing incident: Captain Blood has overhauled a naval vessel, has caused her to drop anchor (on this particular voyage he is sailing with three other ships under his command and a total enlistment of nearly one thousand men) and is now interviewing the arrested captain in his cabin full of marmalade jars and new perukes.

"And what may your name be, sir? If I may ask?"

"Jones, sir."

"What kind of a name is that? English, I take it?"

"No, it's American, sir."

"American? What is an American?"

"America is a new nation among the nations of the world."

"I've not heard of it. Where is it?"

"North of here, north and west. It's a very small nation, at present, and has only been a nation for about two years."

"But the name of your ship is French."

"Yes it is. It is named in honor of Benjamin Franklin, one of our American heroes."

"Bon Homme Richard? What has that to do with Benjamin or Franklin?"

"Well it's an allusion to an almanac Dr. Franklin published called—"

"You weary me, sir. You are captured, American or no, so tell me—do you surrender, with all your men, fittings, cargo and whatever?"

"Sir, I have not yet begun to fight."

"Captain, this is madness. We have you completely surrounded. Furthermore there is a great hole in your hull below the waterline where our warning shot, which was slightly miscalculated, bashed in your timbers. You are taking water at a fearsome rate. And still you wish to fight?"

"It is the pluck of us Americans, sir. We are just that way. Our tiny nation has to be pluckier than most if it is to survive among the bigger, older nations of the world."

"Well, bless my soul. Jones, you are the damnedest goatsucker I ever did see. Stab me if I am not tempted to let you go scot-free, just because of your amazing pluck."

"No sir, I insist on fighting. As founder of the American naval tradition, I must set a good example."

"Jones, return to your vessel and be off."

"No, sir, I will fight to the last shred of canvas, for the honor of America."

"Jones, even in America, wherever it is, you must have encountered the word 'ninny.'"

"Oh. I see. Well then. I think we'll be weighing anchor, Captain, with your permission."

"Choose your occasions, Captain. And God be with you."

Blood, at dawn, a solitary figure pacing the fore-deck. The world of piracy is wide, and at the same time, narrow. One can be gallant all day long, and still end up with a spider monkey for a wife. And what does his mother think of him?

The favorite dance of Captain Blood is the grave and haunting Catalonian *sardana,* in which the participants join hands facing each other to form a ring which gradually becomes larger, then smaller, then larger again. It is danced without smiling, for the most part. He frequently dances this with his men, in the middle of the ocean, after lunch, to the music of a single silver trumpet.

A woman seated on a plain wooden chair under a canopy.
She is wearing white overalls and has a pleased expression
on her face. Watching her, two dogs, German shepherds,
at rest. Behind the dogs, with their backs to us, a row of
naked women kneeling, sitting on their heels, their
buttocks as perfect as eggs or 0's—00 00 00 00 00 00 00.
In profile to the scene, Benvenuto Cellini, in a fur hat.

Two young women wrapped as gifts. The gift-wrapping
is almost indistinguishable from ordinary clothing,
perhaps a shade newer, brighter, more studied than
ordinary clothing. Each young woman holds a white
envelope. Each envelope is addressed to "Tad."

Two young women, naked, tied together by a long red
thread. One is dark, one is fair.

Large (eight by ten feet) sheets of white paper on the
floor, eight of them. The total area covered is about four
hundred square feet; some of the sheets overlap. A string
quartet is playing at one edge of this area, and irregular
rows of formally dressed spectators sit in gilt chairs across
the paper from the players. A large bucket of blue paint
has been placed on the paper. Two young women, naked.
Each has her hair rolled up in a bun; each has been
splashed, breasts, belly, thighs, with blue paint. One, on
her belly, is being dragged across the paper by the other,
who is standing, gripping the first woman's wrists. Their
backs are not painted. Or not painted with. The artist is
Yves Klein.

Nowhere—the middle of it, its exact center. Standing there, a telephone booth, green with tarnished aluminum, the word PHONE and the system's symbol (bell in ring) in medium blue. Inside the telephone booth, two young women, one dark, one fair, facing each other. Their naked breasts and thighs brush lightly (one holding the receiver to the other's ear) as they place calls to their mothers in California. In profile to the scene, at far right, Benvenuto Cellini, wearing white overalls.

Two young men, wrapped as gifts. They have wrapped themselves carefully, tight pants, open-throated shirts, shoes with stacked heels, gold jewelry on right and left wrists, codpieces stuffed with credit cards. They stand, under a Christmas tree big as an office building, and women rush toward them. Or they stand, under a Christmas tree big as an office building, and no women rush toward them. A voice singing Easter songs, hallelujahs.

Georges de La Tour, wearing white overalls (Iron Boy brand) is attending a film. On the screen two young women, naked, are playing Ping-Pong. One makes a swipe with her paddle at a ball the other has placed just over the net and misses, bruising her right leg on the edge of the table. The other puts down her paddle and walks gracefully around the table to examine the hurt; she places her hands on either side of the raw, ugly mark . . . Georges de La Tour picks up his hat and walks from the theatre. In the lobby he purchases a bag of M & Ms which he opens with his teeth.

The world of work: Two young women, one dark, one fair, wearing web belts to which canteens are attached, nothing more. They are sitting side-by-side on high stools (00 00) before a pair of draughting tables, inking-in pencil drawings. Or, in a lumberyard in Southern Illinois, they are unloading a railroad car containing several hundred thousand board feet of Southern yellow pine. Or, in the composing room of a medium-sized Akron daily, they are passing long pieces of paper through a machine which deposits a thin coating of wax on the back side, and then positioning the type on a page. Or, they are driving identical Yellow cabs which are racing side-by-side up Park Avenue with frightened passengers, each driver trying to beat the other to a hole in the traffic. Or, they are seated at adjacent desks in the beige-carpeted area set aside for officers in a bank, refusing loans. Or, they are standing bent over, hands on knees, peering into the site of an archeological dig in the Cameroons. Or, they are teaching, in adjacent classrooms, Naked Physics—in the classroom on the left, Naked Physics I, and in the classroom on the right, Naked Physics II. Or, they are kneeling, sitting on their heels, before a pair of shoeshine stands.

Two young women, wearing web belts to which canteens are attached, nothing more, marching down Broadway again. They are followed by an excited crowd, bands, etc.

Two women, one dark and one fair, wearing parkas, blue wool watch caps on their heads, inspecting a row of naked satyrs, hairy-legged, split-footed, tailed and tufted, who hang from hooks in a meat locker where the temperature is a constant 18 degrees. The women are tickling the satyrs under the tail, where they are most vulnerable, with their long white (nimble) fingers tipped with long curved scarlet nails. The satyrs squirm and dance under this treatment, hanging from hooks, while other women, seated in red plush armchairs, in the meat locker, applaud, or scold, or knit. Hovering near the thermostat, Vladimir Tatlin, in an asbestos tuxedo.

Two women, one dark and one fair, wearing parkas, blue wool watch caps on their heads, inspecting a row of naked young men, hairy-legged, many-toed, pale and shivering, who hang on hooks in a meat locker where the temperature is a constant 18 degrees. The women are tickling the men under the tail, where they are most vulnerable, with their long white (nimble) fingers tipped with long curved scarlet nails. The young men squirm and dance under this treatment, hanging from hooks, while giant eggs, seated in red plush chairs, boil.

Conversations With Goethe

November 13, 1823

I was walking home from the theatre with Goethe this evening when we saw a small boy in a plum-colored waistcoat. Youth, Goethe said, is the silky apple butter on the good brown bread of possibility.

December 9, 1823

Goethe had sent me an invitation to dinner. As I entered his sitting room I found him warming his hands before a cheerful fire. We discussed the meal to come at some length, for the planning of it had been an occasion of earnest thought to him and he was in quite good spirits about the anticipated results, which included sweetbreads prepared in the French manner with celery root and paprika. Food, said Goethe, is the topmost taper on the golden candelabrum of existence.

January 11, 1824

Dinner alone with Goethe. Goethe said, "I will now confide to you some of my ideas about music, something I have been considering for many years. You will have noted that although certain members of the animal kingdom make a kind of music—one speaks of the 'song' of birds, does one not?—no animal known to us takes part in what may be termed an organized musical performance. Man alone does that. I have wondered about crickets—whether their evening cacophony might be considered in this light, as a species of performance, albeit one of little significance to our ears. I have asked Humboldt about it, and Humboldt replied that he thought not, that it is merely a sort of tic on the part of crickets. The great point here, the point that I may choose to enlarge upon in some future work, is not that the members of the animal kingdom do not unite wholeheartedly in this musical way but that man does, to the eternal comfort and glory of his soul."

Music, Goethe said, is the frozen tapioca in the ice chest of History.

March 22, 1824

Goethe had been desirous of making the acquaintance of a young Englishman, a Lieutenant Whitby, then in Weimar on business. I conducted this gentleman to Goethe's house, where Goethe greeted us most cordially and offered us wine and biscuits. English, he said, was a wholly splendid language, which had given him the deepest pleasure over many years. He had mastered it early, he told us, in order to be able to savor the felicities and tragic depths of Shakespeare, with whom no author in the world, before or since, could rightfully be compared. We were in a most pleasant mood and continued to talk about the accomplishments of the young Englishman's countrymen until quite late. The English, Goethe said in parting, are the shining brown varnish on the sad chiffonier of civilization. Lieutenant Whitby blushed most noticeably.

April 7, 1824

When I entered Goethe's house at noon, a wrapped parcel was standing in the foyer. "And what do you imagine this may be?" asked Goethe with a smile. I could not for the life of me fathom what the parcel might contain, for it was most oddly shaped. Goethe explained that it was a sculpture, a gift from his friend van den Broot, the Dutch artist. He unwrapped the package with the utmost care, and I was seized with admiration when the noble figure within was revealed: a representation, in bronze, of a young woman dressed as Diana, her bow bent and an arrow on the string. We marveled together at the perfection of form and fineness of detail, most of all at the indefinable aura of spirituality which radiated from the work. "Truly astonishing!" Goethe exclaimed, and I hastened to agree. Art, Goethe said, is the four per cent interest on the municipal bond of life. He was very pleased with this remark and repeated it several times.

June 18, 1824

Goethe had been having great difficulties with a particular actress at the theatre, a person who conceived that her own notion of how her role was to be played was superior to Goethe's. "It is not enough," he said, sighing, "that I have mimed every gesture for the poor creature, that nothing has been left unexplored in this character I myself have created, willed into being. She persists in what she terms her 'interpretation,' which is ruining the play." He went on to discuss the sorrows of managing a theatre, even the finest, and the exhausting detail that must be attended to, every jot and tittle, if the performances are to be fit for a discriminating public. Actors, he said, are the Scotch weevils in the salt pork of honest effort. I loved him more than ever, and we parted with an affectionate handshake.

September 1, 1824

Today Goethe inveighed against certain critics who had, he said, completely misunderstood Lessing. He spoke movingly about how such obtuseness had partially embittered Lessing's last years, and speculated that it was because Lessing was both critic and dramatist that the attacks had been of more than usual ferocity. Critics, Goethe said, are the cracked mirror in the grand ballroom of the creative spirit. No, I said, they were, rather, the extra baggage on the great cabriolet of conceptual progress. "Eckermann," said Goethe, *"shut up."*

Well we all had our Willie & Wade records 'cept this one guy who was called Spare Some Change? 'cause that's all he ever said and you don't have no Willie & Wade records if the best you can do is Spare Some Change?

So we all took our Willie & Wade records down to the Willie & Wade Park and played all the great and sad Willie & Wade songs on portable players for the beasts of the city, the jumpy black squirrels and burnt-looking dogs and filthy, sick pigeons.

And I thought probably one day Willie or Wade would show up in person at the Willie & Wade Park to check things out, see who was there and what record this person was playing and what record that person was playing.

And probably Willie (or Wade) would just ease around checking things out, saying "Howdy" to this one and that one, and he'd see the crazy black guy in Army clothes who stands in the Willie & Wade Park and every ten minutes, screams like a chicken, and Willie (or Wade) would just say to that guy, "How ya doin' good buddy?" and smile, 'cause strange things don't bother Willie, or Wade, one bit.

And I thought I'd probably go up to Willie then, if it was Willie, and tell him 'bout my friend that died, and how I felt about it at the time, and how I feel about it now. And Willie would say, "I know."

And I would maybe ask him did he remember Galveston, and did he ever when he was a kid play in the old concrete forts along the sea wall with the giant cannon in them that the government didn't want any more, and he'd say, "Sure I did." And I'd say, "You ever work the Blue Jay in San Antone?" and he'd say, "Sure I have."

And I'd say, "Willie, don't them microphones scare you, the ones with the little fuzzy sweaters on them?" And he'd say to me, "They scare me bad, potner, but I don't let on."

And then he (one or the other, Willie or Wade) would say, "Take care, good buddy," and leave the Willie & Wade Park in his black limousine that the driver of had been waiting patiently in all this time, and I would never see him again, but continue to treasure, all my life, his great contributions.

Henrietta and Alexandra

Alexandra was reading Henrietta's manuscript.

"This," she said, pointing with her finger, "is inane."

Henrietta got up and looked over Alexandra's shoulder at the sentence.

"Yes," she said. "I prefer the inane, sometimes. The ane is often inutile to the artist."

There was a moment of contemplation.

"I have been offered a thousand florins for it," Henrietta said. "The Dutch rights."

"How much is that in our money?"

"Two hundred sixty-six dollars."

"Bless Babel," Alexandra said, and took her friend in her arms.

Henrietta said: "Once I was a young girl, very much like any other young girl, interested in the same things, I was exemplary. I was told what I was, that is to say a young girl, and I knew what I was because I had been told and because there were other young girls all around me who had been told the same things and knew the same things, and looking at them and hearing again in my head the things I had been told I knew what a young girl was. We had all been told the same things. I had not been told, for example, that some wine was piss and some not and I had not been told . . . other things. Still I had been told a great many things all very useful but I had not been told that I was going to die in any way that would allow me to realize that I really was going to die and that it would be all over, then, and that this was all there was and that I had damned well better make the most of it. That I discovered for myself and covered with shame and shit as I was I made the most of it. I had not been told how to make the most of it but I figured it out. Then I moved through a period of depression, the depression engendered by the realization that I had placed myself beyond the pale, there I was, beyond the pale. Then I discovered that there were other people beyond the pale with me, that there were quite as many people on the wrong side of the pale as there were on the right side of the pale and that the people on the wrong side of the pale were as complex as the people on the right side of the pale, as unhappy, as subject to time, as subject to death. So what the fuck? I said to myself in the colorful language I had learned on the wrong side of the pale. By this time I was no longer a young girl. I was mature."

Alexandra had a special devotion to the Sacred Heart.

THEORIES OF THE SACRED HEART

LOSS AND RECOVERY OF THE SACRED HEART

CONFLICTING CLAIMS OF THE GREAT CATHE-
DRALS

THE SACRED HEART IN CONTEMPORARY ICO-
NOGRAPHY

APPEARANCE OF SPURIOUS SACRED HEARTS AND
HOW THEY MAY BE DISTINGUISHED FROM
THE TRUE ONE

LOCATION OF THE TRUE SACRED HEART RE-
VEALED

HOW THE ABBÉ ST. GERMAIN PRESERVED THE
TRUE SACRED HEART FROM THE HANDS OF
THE BARBARIANS

WHY THE SACRED HEART IS FREQUENTLY REP-
RESENTED SURMOUNTED BY A CROWN OF
THORNS

MEANING OF THE TINY TONGUE OF FLAME

ORDERS AND CEREMONIES IN THE VENERATION
OF THE SACRED HEART

ROLE OF THE SACRED HEART SOCIETY IN THE
VENERATION OF THE SACRED HEART

Alexandra was also a member of the Knights of St. Dympna, patroness of the insane.

Alexandra and Henrietta were walking down the street in their long gowns. A man looked at them and laughed. Alexandra and Henrietta rushed at him and scratched his eyes out.

As a designer of artificial ruins, Alexandra was well-known. She designed ruins in the manners of Langley, Effner, Robert Adam and Carlo Marchionni, as well as her own manner. She was working on a ruin for a park in Tempe, Arizona, consisting of a ruined wall nicely disintegrated at the top and one end, two classical columns upright and one fallen, vines, and a number of broken urns. The urns were difficult because it was necessary to produce them from intact urns and the workmen at the site were often reluctant to do violence to the urns. Sometimes she pretended to lose her temper. *"Hurl the bloody urn, Umberto!"*

Alexandra looked at herself in the mirror. She admired her breasts, her belly, and her legs, which were, she felt, her best feature.

"Now I will go into the other room and astonish Henrietta, who is also beautiful."

Henrietta stood up and, with a heaving motion, threw the manuscript of her novel into the fire. The manuscript of the novel she had been working on ceaselessly, night and day, for the last ten years.

"Alexandra! Aren't you going to rush to the fire and pull the manuscript of my novel out of it?"

"No."

Henrietta rushed to the fire and pulled the manuscript out of it. Only the first and last pages were fully burned, and luckily, she remembered what was written there.

Henrietta decided that Alexandra did not love her enough. And how could nuances of despair be expressed if you couldn't throw your novel into the fire safely?

Alexandra was sending a petition to Rome. She wanted her old marriage, a dim marriage ten years old to a man named Black Dog, annulled. Alexandra read the rules about sending petitions to Rome to Henrietta.

"All applications to be sent to Rome should be written on good paper, and a double sheet, 8⅛ inches × 10¾ inches, should be employed. The writing of petitions should be done with ink of a good quality, that will remain legible for a long time. Petitions are generally composed in the Latin language, but the use of the French and Italian languages is also permissible.

"The fundamental rule to be observed is that all petitions must be addressed to the Pope, who, directly or indirectly, grants the requested favors. Hence the regulation form of address in all petitions reads *Beatissime Pater*. Following this the petition opens with the customary deferential phrase *ad pedes Sanctitatis Vestrae humillime provolutus*. The concluding formula is indicated by its opening words: *Et Deus* . . . expressing the prayer of blessing which the grateful petitioner addresses in advance to God for the expected favor.

"After introduction, body and conclusion of the petition have been duly drawn, the sheet is evenly folded length-wise, and on its back, to the right of the fold line, are indited the date of the presentation and the petitioner's name.

"The presentation of petitions is generally made through an agent, whose name is inscribed in the right-hand corner on the back of the petition. This signature is necessary because the agent will call for the grant, and the Congregations deliver rescripts to no one but the agent whose name is thus recorded. The agents, furthermore, pay the fee and taxes for the requested rescripts of favor, give any necessary explanations and comments that may be required, and are at all times in touch with the authorities in order to correct any mistakes or defects in the petitions. Between the hours of nine and one o'clock the agents gather in the offices of the Curial administration to hand in new petitions and to inquire about the fate of those not yet decided. Many of them also go to the anterooms of secretaries in order to discuss important matters personally with the leading officials.

"For lay persons it is as a rule useless to forward petitions through the mails to the Roman Congregations, because as a matter of principle they will not be considered. Equally useless, of course, would be the enclosing of postage stamps with such petitions. Applications by telegraph are not permitted because of their publicity. Nor are decisions ever given by telegraph."

Alexandra stopped reading.

"Jesus Christ!" Henrietta said.

"This wine is piss," Alexandra said.

"You needn't drink it then."

"I'll have another glass."

"You wanted me to buy California wine," Henrietta said.

"But there's no reason to buy absolute vinegar is there? I mean couldn't you have asked the man at the store?"

"They don't always tell the truth."

"I remember that time in Chicago," Alexandra said. "That was a good bottle. And afterwards . . ."

"How much did we pay for that bottle?" Henrietta asked, incuriously.

"Twelve dollars. Or ten dollars. Ten or twelve."

"The hotel," Henrietta said. "Snapdragons on the night table."

"You were . . . exquisite."

"I was mature," Henrietta said.

"If you were mature then, what are you now?"

"More mature," Henrietta said. "Maturation is a process that is ongoing."

"When are you old?" Alexandra asked.

"Not while love is here," Henrietta said.

Henrietta said: "Now I am mature. In maturity I found a rich world beyond the pale and found it possible to live in that world with a degree of enthusiasm. My mother says I am deluded but I have stopped talking to my mother. My father is dead and thus has no opinion. Alexandra continues to heap up indulgences by exclaiming 'Jesus, Mary and Joseph!' which is worth an indulgence of fifty days each time it is exclaimed. Some of the choicer ejaculations are worth seven years and seven quarantines and these she pursues with the innocent cupidity of the small investor. She keeps her totals in a little book. I love her. She has to date worked off eighteen thousand years in the flames of Purgatory. I tell her that the whole thing is a shuck but she refuses to consider my views on this point. Alexandra is immature in that she thinks she will live forever, live after she is dead at the right hand of God in His glory with His power and His angels and His whatnot and I cannot persuade her otherwise. Joseph Conrad will live forever but Alexandra will not. I love her. Now we are going out."

Henrietta and Alexandra went walking. They were holding each other's arms. Alexandra moved a hand sensuously with a circular motion around one of Henrietta's breasts. Henrietta did the same thing to Alexandra. People were looking at them with strange expressions on their faces. They continued walking, under the shaped trees of the boulevard. They were swooning with pleasure, more or less. Someone called the police.

Speaking of the human body, Klee said: One bone alone achieves nothing.

Pondering this, people placed lamps on all of the street corners, and sofas next to the lamps. People sat on the sofas and read Spinoza there, an interesting glare cast on the pages by the dithering inconstant traffic lights. At other points, on the street, four-poster beds were planted, and loving couples slept or watched television together, the sets connected to the empty houses behind them by long black cables. Elsewhere, on the street, conversation pits were chipped out of the concrete, floored with Adam rugs, and lengthy discussions were held. Do we really need a War College? *was a popular subject. Favorite paintings were lashed to the iron railings bordering the sidewalks, a Gainsborough, a van Dongen, a perfervid evocation of Umbrian mental states, an important dark-brown bruising of Arches paper by a printer of modern life.*

One man hung all of his shirts on the railing bordering a sidewalk, he had thirty-nine, and another was brushing his teeth in his bathrobe, another was waxing his fine moustache, a woman was marking cards with a little prickly roller so that her husband, the gambler, would win forever. A man said, "Say, mon, fix me some of dem chitlins you fry so well," and another man said, "Howard, my son, I am now going to show you how to blow glass"— he dipped his glass-blowing tube into a furnace of bubbling glass, there on the street, and blew a rathskeller of beer glasses, each goldenly full.

Inside the abandoned houses subway trains rushed in both directions and genuine nameless animals ate each other with ghastly fervor—

Monday. Many individuals are grasping hold of the sewer grates with both hands, a manifestation, in the words of S. Moholy-Nagy, of the tragic termination of the will to fly.

The Sea of Hesitation

"If Jackson had pressed McClellan in White Oak Swamp," Francesca said. "If Longstreet had proceeded vigorously on the first day at Second Manassas. If we had had the 40,000 pairs of shoes we needed when we entered Maryland. If Bloss had not found the envelope containing the two cigars and the copy of Lee's Secret Order No. 191 at Frederick. If the pneumonia had not taken Jackson. If Ewell had secured possession of Cemetery Heights on the first day of Gettysburg. If Pickett's charge . . . If Early's march into the Valley . . . If we had had sufficient food for our troops at Petersburg. If our attack on Fort Stedman had succeeded. If Pickett and Fitzhugh Lee had not indulged in a shad bake at Five Forks. If there had been stores and provisions as promised at Amelia Court House. If Ewell had not been captured at Saylor's Creek together with sixteen artillery pieces and four hundred wagons. If Lee had understood Lincoln—his mind, his larger intentions. If there had been a degree of competence in our civilian administration equal to that exhibited by the military. Then, perhaps, matters would have been brought to a happier conclusion."

"Yes," I said.

Francesca is slightly obsessed. But one must let people talk about what they want to talk about. One must let people do what they want to do.

This morning in the mail I received an abusive letter from a woman in Prague.

Dear Greasy Thomas:
You cannot understand what a pig you are. You are a pig, you idiot. You think you understand things but there is nothing you understand, nothing, idiot pig-swine. You have not wisdom and you have no discretion and nothing can be done without wisdom and discretion. How did a pig-cretin like yourself ever wriggle into life? Why do you exist still, vulgar swine? If you don't think I am going to inform the government of your inappropriate continued existence, a stain on the country's face . . . You can expect Federal Marshals in clouds very soon, cretin-hideous-swine, and I will laugh as they haul you away in their green vans, ugly toad. You know nothing about anything, garbage-face, and the idea that you would dare "think" for others (I know you are not capable of "feeling") is so wildly outrageous that I would laugh out loud if I were not sick of your importunate posturing, egregious fraud-pig. You are not even an honest pig which is at least of some use in the world, you are rather an ocean of pig-dip poisoning everything you touch. I do not like you at all.

Love,
Jinka

I read the letter twice. She is certainly angry. But one must let people do what they want to do.

I work for the City. In the Human Effort Administration. My work consists of processing applications. People apply for all sorts of things. I approve all applications and buck them upwards, where they are usually disapproved. Upstairs they do not agree with me, that people should be permitted to do what they want to do. Upstairs they have different ideas. But "different ideas" are welcomed, in my particular cosmos.

Before I worked for the City I was interested in changing behavior. I thought behavior could be changed. I had a B.A. in psychology, was working on an M.A. I was into sensory deprivation. I did sensory deprivation studies for a while at McGill and later at Princeton.

At McGill we inhabited the basement of Taub Hall, believed to be the first building in the world devoted exclusively to the study of hatred. But we were not studying hatred, we were doing black-box work and the hatred people kindly lent us their basement. I was in charge of the less intelligent subjects (the subjects were divided into less intelligent and more intelligent). I spent two years in the basement of Taub Hall and learned many interesting things.

The temperature of the head does not decrease in sleep. The temperature of the rest of the body does.

There I sat for weeks on end monitoring subjects who had half Ping-Pong balls taped over their eyes and a white-noise generator at 40db singing in their ears. I volunteered as a subject and, gratified at being assigned to the "more intelligent" group, spent many many hours in the black box with half

Ping-Pong balls taped over my eyes and the white-noise generator emitting its obliterating whine/whisper. Although I had some intricate Type 4 hallucinations, nothing much else happened to me. Except . . . I began to wonder if behavior *should be* changed. That there was "behavior" at all seemed to me a small miracle.

I pondered going on to stress theory, wherein one investigates the ways in which the stressed individual reacts to stress, but decided suddenly to do something else instead. I decided to take a job with the Human Effort Administration and to try, insofar as possible, to let people do what they want to do.

I am aware that my work is, in many ways, meaningless.

A call from Honor, my ex-wife. I've promised her a bed for her new apartment.

"Did you get it?"

"Not yet."

"Why not?"

"I've been busy. Doing things."

"But what about the bed?"

"I told you I'd take care of it."

"Yes but when?"

"Some people can get their own beds for their new apartments."

"But that's not the point. You promised."

"That was in the first flush of good feeling and warmth. When you said you were coming back to town."

"Now you don't have any good feeling and warmth?"

"Full of it. Brimming. How's Sam?"

"He's getting tired of sleeping on the couch. It's not big enough for both of us."

"My heart cries out for him."

She's seeing Sam now, that's a little strange. She didn't seem to take to him, early on.

Sam. What's he like? Like a villain. Hair like an oil spill, mustache like a twist of carbon paper, high white lineless forehead, black tights and doublet, dagger clasped in treacherous right hand, sneaks when he's not slithering. . . .

No. That's incompletely true. Sam's just like the rest of us: jeans, turtleneck, beard, smile with one chipped tooth, good with children, backward in his taxes, a degree in education, a B.Ed. And he came with the very best references too, Charlotte doted, Francine couldn't get enough, Mary Jo chased him through Grand Central with the great whirling loop of her lariat, causing talk— But Honor couldn't see him, in the beginning. She's reconsidered. I wish she hadn't thrown the turntable on the floor, a $600 B & O, but all that's behind us now.

I saw this morning that the building at the end of the street's been sold. It stood empty for years, an architectural anomaly, three-storied, brick, but most of all, triangular. Two streets come together in a point there, and prospective buyers must have boggled at the angles. I judged that the owners decided to let morality go hang and sold to a *ménage à trois*. They'll need a triple bed, customized to fit those odd corners. I can see them with protractor and Skilsaw, getting the thing just right. Then sweeping up the bedcrumbs.

She telephones again.

"It doesn't have to be the best bed in the world. Any old bed will do. Sam's bitching all night long."

"For you, dear friend, I'll take every pain. We're checking now in Indonesia, a rare albino bed's been sighted there . . ."

"Tom, this isn't funny. I slept in the bathtub last night."

"You're too long for the bathtub."

"Do you want Sam to do it?"

Do I want Sam to do it?

"No. I'll do it."

"Then *do* it."

We were content for quite a while, she taught me what she'd majored in, a lovely Romance tongue, we visited the country and when I'd ask in a pharmacie for a razor they'd give me rosewater. I'm teasing her, and she me. She wants Sam. That's good.

Francesca was reading to me.

"This is the note Lee wrote," she said. "Listen. 'No one is more aware than myself of my inability for the duties of my position. I cannot even accomplish what I myself desire. How can I fulfill the expectations of others? In addition I sensibly feel the growing failure of my bodily strength. I have not yet recovered from the attack I experienced the past spring. I am becoming more and more incapable of exertion, and am thus prevented from making the personal examinations and giving the personal supervision to the operations in the field which I feel to be necessary. I am so dull making use of the eyes of others I am frequently misled. Everything, therefore, points to the advantages to be derived from a new commander. A younger and abler man than myself can readily be obtained. I know that he will have as gallant and brave an army as ever existed to second his efforts, and it would be the happiest day of my life to see at its head a worthy . . .'"

Francesca stopped reading.

"That was *Robert E. Lee*," she said.

"Yes," I said.

"The leader of all the armies of the Confederacy,"
she said.

"I know."

"I wanted him to win. So much."

"I understand."

"But he did not."

"I have read about it."

Francesca has Confederate-gray eyes which re-
flect, mostly, a lifelong contemplation of the nobility
of Lee's great horse, Traveller. I left Francesca and
walked in the park, where I am afraid to walk, after
dark. One must let people do what they want to do,
but what if they want to slap you upside the head
with a Stillson wrench and take the credit cards out
of your pockets? A problem.

The poor are getting poorer. I saw a poor man
and asked him if he had any money.

"Money?" he said. "Money thinks I died a long
time ago."

We have moved from the Age of Anxiety to the
Age of Fear. This is of course progress, psychologi-
cally speaking. I intend no irony.

Another letter from Jinka.

> Undear Thomas:
> The notion that only man is vile must have been
> invented to describe you, vile friend. I cannot
> contain the revulsion that whelms in me at the
> sight of your name, in the Prague telephone
> book, from your time in Prague. I have
> scratched it out of my copy, and scratched it out
> of all the copies I could get my hands on, in
> telephone booths everywhere. This symbolic re-
> moval of you from the telephone booths of our
> ancient city should not escape your notice, stink-
> ing meat. You have been erased and the anoint-
> ment of the sick, formerly known as Extreme

Unction, also as the Last Rites, is what I have in mind for you, soon. Whatever you are doing, stop it, drear pig. The insult to consciousness afforded by your project, whatever it is, cannot be suffered gladly, and I for one do not intend to so suffer. I have measures not yet in the books, and will take them. What I have in mind is not shallots and fresh rosemary, gutless wonder, and your continued association with that ridiculously thin Robert E. Lee girl has not raised you in my esteem, not a bit. One if by land and two if by sea, and it will be sudden, I promise you. Be afraid.

Cordially,
Jinka

I put this letter with the others, clipped together with a paper clip. How good writing such letters must make her feel!

Wittgenstein was I think wrong when he said that about that which we do not know, we should not speak. He closed by fiat a great amusement park, there. Nothing gives me more pleasure than speaking about that which I do not know. I am not sure whether my ideas about various matters are correct or incorrect, but speak about them I must.

I decided to call my brother in San Francisco. He is a copy editor on the *San Francisco Chronicle* (although he was trained as a biologist—he is doing what he wants to do, more or less). Because we are both from the South our conversations tend to be conducted in jiveass dialect.

"Hey," I said.

"Hey," he said.

"What's happening? You got any girl copy boys on that newspaper yet?"

"Man," Paul said, "we got not only girl copy boys we got *topless* girl copy boys. We gonna hire us a reporter next week. They promised us."

"That's wonderful," I said. "How are you feeling?"

"I'm depressed."

"Is it specific or nonspecific?"

"Well," Paul said, "I have to read the paper a lot. I'm ready to drop the bomb. On us."

One must let people do what they want to do. Fortunately my brother has little to say about when and where the bomb will be dropped.

My other friend is Catherine. Catherine, like Francesca, is hung up on the past. She is persuaded that in an earlier existence she was Balzac's mistress (one of Balzac's mistresses).

"I endured Honoré's grandness," she said, "because it was spurious. Spurious grandness I understand very well. What I could not understand was his hankering for greatness."

"But he *was* great," I said.

"I was impatient with all those artists, sitting around, hankering for greatness. Of course Honoré was great. But he didn't know it, at the time, for sure. Or he did and he didn't. There were moments of doubt, depression."

"As is natural."

"The seeking after greatness," said Catherine, "is a sickness, in my opinion. It is like greed, only greed has better results. Greed can at least bring you a fine house on a grand avenue, and strawberries for breakfast, in a rich cream, and servants to beat, when they do not behave. I *prefer* greed. Honoré was greedy, in a reasonable way, but what he was mostly interested in was greatness. I was stuck with greatness."

"Yes," I said.

"You," Catherine said, "are neither great nor greedy."

"One must let people be—" I began.

"Yes," Catherine said, "that sounds good, on the surface, but thinking it through—" She finished her espresso, placed the little cup precisely on the little saucer. "Take me out," she said. "Take me to a library."

We went to a library and spent a pleasant afternoon there.

Francesca was stroking the brown back of a large spayed cat—the one that doesn't like me.

"Lee was not without his faults," she said. "Not for a moment would I have you believe that he was faultless."

"What was his principal fault?"

"Losing," she said.

I went to the Art Cinema and saw a Swedish film about a man living alone on an island. Somebody was killing a great many sheep on the island and the hero, a hermit, was suspected. There were a great many shots of sheep with their throats cut, red blood on the white snow, glimpses. The hermit fixed a car for a woman whose car had broken down. They went to bed together. There were flashbacks having to do with the woman's former husband, a man in a wheelchair. It was determined that somebody else, not the hermit, had been killing the sheep. The film ended with a car crash in which the woman was killed. Whiteout.

Should great film artists be allowed to do what they want to do?

Catherine is working on her translation of the complete works of Balzac. Honoré, she insists, has never been properly translated. She will devote her life to the task, she says. Actually I have looked at some pages of her *Louis Lambert* and they seem to me significantly worse than the version I read in college. I think of Balzac in the great statue by Rodin, holding his erect (possibly overstated) cock in both hands under his cloak of bronze. An inspiration.

When I was in the black box, during my SD days, there was nothing I wanted to do. I didn't even want to get out. Or perhaps there was one thing I wanted to do: Sit in the box with the half Ping-Pong balls taped over my eyes and the white-noise generator standing in for the sirens of Ulysses (himself an early SD subject) and permit the Senior Investigator (Dr. Colcross, the one with the bad leg) to do what *he* wanted to do.

Is this will-lessness, finally? Abulia, as we call it in the trade? I don't think so.

I pursue Possibility. That's something.

There is no moment that exceeds in beauty that moment when one looks at a woman and finds that she is looking at you in the same way that you are looking at her. The moment in which she bestows that look that says, "Proceed with your evil plan, sumbitch." The initial smash of glance on glance. Then, the drawing near. This takes a long time, it seems like months, although only minutes pass, in fact. Languor is the word that describes this part of the process. Your persona floats toward her persona, over the Sea of Hesitation. Many weeks pass before they meet, but the weeks are days, or seconds. Still, everything is decided. You have slept together in the glance.

She takes your arm and you leave the newsstand, walking very close together, so that your side brushes her side lightly. Desire is here a very strong factor, because you are weak with it, and the woman is too, if she has any sense at all (but of course she is a sensible woman, and brilliant and witty and hungry as well). So, on the sidewalk outside the newsstand, you stand for a moment thinking about where to go, at eleven o'clock in the morning, and here it is, in the sunlight, that you take the first good look at her, and she at you, to see if either one has any hideous blemish that has been overlooked, in the first rush of good feeling. There are none. None. No blemishes (except those spiritual blemishes that will be discovered later, after extended acquaintance, and which none of us are without, but which are now latent? dormant? in any case, not visible on the surface, at this time). Everything is fine. And so, with renewed confidence, you begin to walk, and to seek a place where you might sit down, and have a drink, and talk a bit, and fall into each other's eyes, temporarily, and find some pretzels, and have what is called a conversation, and tell each other what you think is true about the world, and speak of the strange places where each of you has been (Surinam, in her case, where she bought the belt she is wearing, Lima in your case, where you contracted telegraph fever), and make arrangements for your next meeting (both of you drinking Scotch and water, at eleven in the morning, and you warm to her because of her willingness to leave her natural mid-morning track, for you), and make, as I say, arrangements for your next meeting, which must be this very night! or you both will die—

There is no particular point to any of this behavior. Or: This behavior is the only behavior which has point. Or: There is some point to this behavior but this behavior is not the only behavior which has point. Which is true? Truth is greatly overrated, volition where it exists must be protected, wanting itself can be obliterated, some people have forgotten how to want.

When he came to look at the building, with a real-estate man hissing and oozing beside him, we lowered the blinds, muted or extinguished lights, threw newspapers and dirty clothes on the floor in piles, burned rubber bands in ashtrays, and played Buxtehude on the hi-fi—shaking organ chords whose vibrations made the plaster falling from the ceiling fall faster. The new owner stood in profile, refusing to shake hands or even speak to us, a tall thin young man suited in hopsacking with a large manila envelope under one arm. We pointed to the plaster, to crevasses in the walls, sagging ceilings, leaks. Nevertheless, he closed.

Soon he was slipping little rent bills into the mailboxes, slip slip slip slip slip. In sixteen years we'd never had rent bills but now we have rent bills. He's raised the rent, and lowered the heat. The new owner creeps into the house by night and takes the heat away with him. He wants us out, out. If we were gone, the building would be decontrolled. The rents would climb into the air like steam.

Bicycles out of the halls, says the new owner. Shopping carts out of the halls. My halls.

The new owner stands in profile in the street in front of our building. He looks up the street, then down the street—this wondrous street where our friends and neighbors live in Christian, Jewish, and, in some instances, Islamic peace. The new owner is writing the Apartments Unfurn. ads of the future, in his head.

The new owner fires the old super, simply because the old super is a slaphappy, widowed, shot-up, black, Korean War-sixty-five-per-cent-disability-vet drunk. There is a shouting confrontation in the basement. The new owner threatens the old super with the police. The old super is locked out. A new super is hired who does not put out the garbage, does not mop the halls, does not, apparently, exist. Roaches prettyfoot into the building because the new owner has stopped the exerminating service. The new owner wants us out.

We whisper to the new owner, through the walls. Go away! Own something else! Don't own this building! Try the Sun Belt! Try Alaska, Hawaii! Sail away, new owner, sail away!

The new owner arrives, takes out his keys, opens the locked basement. The new owner is standing in the basement, owning the basement, with its single dangling bare bulb and the slightly busted souvenirs of all our children's significant progress. He is taking away the heat, carrying it out with him under his coat, a few pounds at a time, and bringing in with him, a few hundred at a time, his hired roaches.

The new owner stands in the hall, his manila envelope under his arm, owning the hall.

The new owner wants our apartment, and the one below, and the two above, and the one above them. He's a bachelor, tall thin young man in cheviot, no wife, no children, only buildings. He's covered the thermostat with a locked clear-plastic case. His manila envelope contains estimates and floor plans and draft Apartments Unfurn. ads and documents from the Office of Rent and Housing Preservation which speak of Maximum Base Rents and Maximum Collectible Rents and under what circumstances a Senior Citizen Rent Increase Exemption Order may be voided.

Black handprints all over the green of the halls where the new owner has been feeling the building.

The new owner has informed the young cohabiting couple on the floor above us (rear) that they are illegally living in sin and that for this reason he will give them only a month-to-month lease, so that at the end of each and every month they must tremble.

The new owner has informed the old people in the apartment above us (front) that he is prepared to prove that they do not actually live in their apartment in that they are old and so do not, in any real sense, live, and are thus subject to a Maximum Real Life Estimate Revision, which, if allowed by the City, will award him their space. Levon and Priscilla tremble.

The new owner stands on the roof, where the tomato plants are, owning the roof. May a good wind blow him to Hell.

Terminus

She agrees to live with him for "a few months"; where? probably at the Hotel Terminus, which is close to the Central Station, the blue coaches leaving for Lyons, Munich, the outerlands . . . Of course she has a Gold Card, no, it was not left at the florist's, absolutely not . . .

The bellmen at the Hotel Terminus find the new arrival odd, even furtive; her hair is cut in a funny way, wouldn't you call it funny? and her habits are nothing but odd, the incessant pumping of the huge accordion, "Malagueña" over and over again, at the hour usually reserved for dinner . . .

The yellow roses are delivered, no, white baby orchids, the cream-colored walls of the room are severe and handsome, tall windows looking down the avenue toward the Angel-Garden. Kneeling, with a sterilized needle, she removes a splinter from his foot; he's thinking, *clothed, and in my right mind,* and she says, now I lay me down to sleep, I mean it, Red Head—

They've agreed to meet on a certain street corner; when he arrives, early, she rushes at him from a doorway; it's cold, she's wearing her long black coat, it's too thin for this weather; he gives her his scarf, which she wraps around her head like a babushka; tell me, she says, how did this happen?

When she walks, she slouches, or skitters, or skids, catches herself and stands with one hip tilted and a hand on the hip, like a cowboy; she's twenty-six, served three years in the Army, didn't like it and got out, took a degree in statistics and worked for an insurance company, didn't like it and quit and fell in love with him and purchased the accordion . . .

Difficult, he says, difficult, difficult, but she is trying to learn "When Irish Eyes Are Smiling," the sheet music propped on the cream marble mantelpiece, in two hours' time the delightful psychiatrist will be back from his Mexican vacation, which he spent in perfect dread, speaking to spiders—

Naked, she twists in his arms to listen to a sound outside the door, a scratching, she freezes, listening; he's startled by the beauty of her tense back, the raised shoulders, tilted head, there's nothing, she turns to look at him, what does she see? The telephone rings, it's the delightful psychiatrist (hers), singing the praises of Cozumel, Cancun . . .

He punches a hole in a corner of her Gold Card and hangs it about her neck on a gold chain.

What are they doing in this foreign city? She's practicing "Cherokee," and he's plotting his next move, up, out, across, down . . . He's hired in Flagstaff, at a succulent figure, more consulting, but he doesn't want to do that any more, they notice a sullen priest reading his breviary in the Angel-Garden, she sits on a bench and opens the *Financial Times* (in which his letter to the editor has been published, she consumes it with intense comprehension), only later, after a game of billiards, does he begin telling her how beautiful she is, no, she says, no, no—

I'll practice for eighteen hours a day, she says, stopping only for a little bread soaked in wine; he gathers up the newspapers, including the *Financial Times,* and stacks them neatly on the cream-colored radiator; and in the spring, he says, I'll be going away.

She's setting the table and humming "Vienna"; yes, she says, it will be good to have you gone.

They're so clearly in love that cops wave at them from passing cruisers; what has happened to his irony, which was supposed to protect him, keep him clothed, and in his right mind? I love you so much, so much, she says, and he believes her, sole in a champagne sauce, his wife is skiing in Chile—

And while you sit by the fire, tatting, he says . . .

She says, no tatting for me, Big Boy . . .

In the night, he says, alone, to see of me no more, your good fortune.

Police cars zip past the Hotel Terminus in threes, sirens hee-hawing . . .

No one has told him that he is *a husband;* he has learned nothing from the gray in his hair; the additional lenses in the lenses of his spectacles have not educated him; the merriment of dental assistants has not brought him the news; he behaves as if *something* were possible, still; there's whispering at the Hotel Terminus.

He decides to go to a bar and she screams at him, music from the small radio, military marches, military waltzes; she's confused, she says, she really didn't mean that, but meant, rather, that the bell captain at the Hotel Terminus had said something she thought offensive, something about "Malagueña," it was not the words but the tone—

Better make the bed, he says, the bed in which you'll sleep, chaste and curly, when I'm gone . . .

Yes, she says, yes that's what they say . . .

True, he's lean; true, he's not entirely stupid; yes, he's given up cigarettes; yes, he's given up saying "forgive me," no longer uses the phrase "as I was saying"; he's mastered backgammon and sleeping with the radio on; he's apologized for his unkind remark about the yellow-haired young man at whom she was not staring— And when a lover drifts off while being made love to, it's a lesson in humility, right?

He looks at the sleeping woman; how beautiful she is! He touches her back, lightly.

The psychiatrist, learned elf, calls and invites them to his party, to be held in the Palm Room of the Hotel Terminus, patients will dance with doctors, doctors will dance with receptionists, receptionists will dance with detail men, a man who once knew Ferenczi will be there in a sharkskin suit, a motorized wheelchair— Yes, says the psychiatrist, *of course* you can play "Cherokee," and for an encore, anything of Victor Herbert's—

She, grimly: I don't like to try to make nobody bored, Hot Stuff.

Warlike music in all hearts, she says, why are we together?

But on the other hand, she says, *that which exists is more perfect than that which does not* . . .

This is absolutely true. He is astonished by the quotation. In the Hotel Terminus coffee shop, he holds her hand tightly.

Thinking of getting a new nightie, she says, maybe a dozen.

Oh? he says.

He's a whistling dog this morning, brushes his teeth with tequila thinking about *Geneva,* she, dying of love, shoves him up against a cream-colored wall, biting at his shoulders . . . Little teed off this morning, aren't you, babe? he says, and she says, fixin' to prepare to get mad, way I'm bein' treated, and he says, oh darlin', and she says, way I'm bein' jerked around—

Walking briskly in a warm overcoat toward the Hotel Terminus, he stops to buy flowers, yellow freesias, and wonders what "a few months" can mean: three, eight? He has fallen out of love this morning, feels a refreshing distance, an absolution— But then she calls him *amigo,* as she accepts the flowers, and says, *not bad, Red Head,* and he falls back into love again, forever. She comes toward him fresh from the bath, opens her robe. Goodbye, she says, goodbye.

The first thing the baby did wrong was to tear pages out of her books. So we made a rule that each time she tore a page out of a book she had to stay alone in her room for four hours, behind the closed door. She was tearing out about a page a day, in the beginning, and the rule worked fairly well, although the crying and screaming from behind the closed door were unnerving. We reasoned that that was the price you had to pay, or part of the price you had to pay. But then as her grip improved she got to tearing out two pages at a time, which meant eight hours alone in her room, behind the closed door, which just doubled the annoyance for everybody. But she wouldn't quit doing it. And then as time went on we began getting days when she tore out three or four pages, which put her alone in her room for as much as sixteen hours at a stretch, interfering with normal feeding and worrying my wife. But I felt that if you made a rule you had to stick to it, had to be consistent, otherwise they get the wrong idea. She was about fourteen months old or fifteen months old at that point. Often, of course, she'd go to sleep, after an hour or so of yelling, that was a mercy. Her room was very nice, with a nice wooden rocking horse and practically a hundred dolls and stuffed animals. Lots of things to do in that room if you used your time wisely, puzzles and things. Unfortunately sometimes when we opened the door we'd find that she'd torn more pages out of more books while she was inside, and these pages had to be added to the total, in fairness.

The baby's name was Born Dancin'. We gave the baby some of our wine, red, white, and blue, and spoke seriously to her. But it didn't do any good.

I must say she got real clever. You'd come up to her where she was playing on the floor, in those rare times when she was out of her room, and there'd be a book there, open beside her, and you'd inspect it and it would look perfectly all right. And then you'd look closely and you'd find a page that had one little corner torn, could easily pass for ordinary wear-and-tear but I knew what she'd done, she'd torn off this little corner and swallowed it. So that had to count and it did. They will go to any lengths to thwart you. My wife said that maybe we were being too rigid and that the baby was losing weight. But I pointed out to her that the baby had a long life to live and had to live in the world with others, had to live in a world where there were many, many rules, and if you couldn't learn to play by the rules you were going to be left out in the cold with no character, shunned and ostracized by everyone. The longest we ever kept her in her room consecutively was eighty-eight hours, and that ended when my wife took the door off its hinges with a crowbar even though the baby still owed us twelve hours because she was working off twenty-five pages. I put the door back on its hinges and added a big lock, one that opened only if you put a magnetic card in a slot, and I kept the card.

But things didn't improve. The baby would come out of her room like a bat out of hell and rush to the nearest book, **Goodnight Moon** *or whatever, and begin tearing pages out of it hand over fist. I mean there'd be thirty-four pages of* **Goodnight Moon** *on the floor in ten seconds. Plus the covers. I began to get a little worried. When I added up her indebtedness, in terms of hours, I could see that she wasn't going to get out of her room until 1992, if then. Also, she was looking pretty wan. She hadn't been to* the park in weeks. We had more or less of an ethical crisis on our hands.

I solved it by declaring that it was all right to tear pages out of books, and moreover, that it was all right to have torn pages out of books in the past. That is one of the satisfying things about being a parent—you've got a lot of moves, each one good as gold. The baby and I sit happily on the floor, side by side, tearing pages out of books, and sometimes, just for fun, we go out on the street and smash a windshield together.

The Mothball Fleet

It was early morning, just after dawn, in fact. The mothball fleet was sailing down the Hudson. Grayish-brown shrouds making odd shapes at various points on the superstructures. I counted forty destroyers, four light cruisers, two heavy cruisers, and a carrier. A fog lay upon the river.

I went aboard as the fleet reached the Narrows. I noticed a pair of jeans floating on the surface of the water, stiff with paint. I abandoned my small outboard and jumped for the ladder of the lead destroyer.

There was no one on deck. All of the gun mounts and some pieces of special equipment were coated with a sort of plastic webbing, which had a slightly repellent feeling when touched. I watched my empty Pacemaker bobbing in the heavy wake of the fleet. I called out. "Hello! Hello!"

Behind us, the vessels were disposed in fleet formation—the carrier in the center, the two heavy cruisers before and behind her, the destroyer screen correctly placed in relation to the cruisers, or as much so as the width of the channel would allow. We were making, I judged, ten to twelve knots.

There was no other traffic on the water; this I thought strange.

It was now about six-thirty; the fog was breaking up, a little. I decided to climb to the bridge. I entered the wheelhouse; there was no one at the wheel. I took the wheel in my hands, tried to turn it a point or two, experimentally; it was locked in place.

A man entered from the chartroom behind me. He immediately walked over to me and removed my hands from the wheel.

He wore a uniform, but it seemed more a steward's or barman's dress than a naval officer's. His face was not unimpressive: dark hair carefully brushed, a strong nose, good mouth and chin. I judged him to be in his late fifties. He re-entered the chartroom. I followed him.

"May I ask where this . . ."

"Mothball fleet," he supplied.

"—is bound?"

He did not answer my question. He was looking at a chart.

"If it's a matter of sealed orders or something . . ."

"No no," he said, without looking up. "Nothing like that." Then he said, "A bit careless with your little boat, aren't you?"

This made me angry. "Not normally. On the contrary. But something—"

"Of course," he said. "You were anticipated. Why d'you think that ladder wasn't secured?"

I thought about this for a moment. I decided to shift the ground of the conversation slightly.

"Are there crews aboard the other ships?"

"No," he said. I felt however that he had appreciated my shrewdness in guessing that there were no crews aboard the other ships.

"Radio?" I asked. "Remote control or something?"

"Something like that," he said.

The forty destroyers, four light cruisers, two heavy cruisers, and the carrier were moving in perfect formation toward the open sea. The sight was a magnificent one. I had been in the Navy—two years as a supply officer in New London, principally.

"Is this a test of some kind?" I asked. "New equipment or—"

"You're afraid that we'll be used for target practice? Hardly." He seemed momentarily amused.

"No. But ship movements on this scale—"

"It was difficult," he said. He then walked out of the chartroom and seated himself in one of the swivel chairs on posts in front of the bridge windows. I followed him.

"May I ask your rank?"

"Why not ask my name?"

"All right."

"I am the Admiral."

I looked again at his uniform which suggested no such thing.

"Objectively," he said, smiling slightly.

"My name is—" I began.

"I am not interested in your name," he said. "I am only interested in your behavior. As you can see, I have at my disposal forty-seven brigs, of which the carrier's is the most comfortable. Not that I believe you will behave other than correctly. At the moment, I want you to do this: Go down to the galley and make a pot of coffee. Make sandwiches. You may make one for yourself. Then bring them here." He settled back in his seat and regarded the calm, even sea.

"All right," I said. "Yes."

"You will say: 'Yes, sir,'" he corrected me.

"Yes, sir."

I wandered about the destroyer until I found the galley. I made the coffee and sandwiches and returned with them to the bridge.

The "Admiral" drank his coffee silently. Seabirds made passes at the mast where the radar equipment, I saw, was covered with the same plastic material that enclosed the gun installations.

"What is that stuff used for the mothballing?" I asked.

"It's a polyvinylchloride solution which also contains vinyl acetate," he said. "It's sprayed on and then hardens. If you were to cut it open you'd find inside, around the equipment, four or five small cloth bags containing silicate of soda in crystals, to absorb moisture. A very neat system. It does just what it's supposed to do, keeps the equipment good as new."

He had finished his sandwich. A bit of mustard had soiled the sleeve of his white coat, which had gold epaulets. I thought again that he most resembled not an admiral but a man from whom one would order drinks.

"What is your mission?" I asked, determined not to be outfaced by a man with mustard on his coat.

"To be at sea," he said.

"Only that?"

"Think a bit," he said. "Think first of shipyards. Think of hundreds of thousands of men in shipyards, on both coasts, building these ships. Think of the welders, the pipefitters, the electricians, naval architects, people in the Bureau of the Budget. Think of the launchings, each with its bottle of champagne on a cord of plaited ribbons hurled at the bow by the wife of some high official. Think of the first sailors coming aboard, the sea trials, the captains for whom a particular ship was a first command. Each ship has a history, no ship is without its history. Think of the six-inch guns shaking a particular ship as they were fired, the jets leaving the deck of the carrier at tightly spaced intervals, the maneuvering of the cruisers during this or that engagement, the damage taken. Think of each ship's log faithfully kept over the years, think of the Official Naval History which now runs, I am told, to three hundred some-odd very large volumes.

"And then," he said, "think of each ship moving up the Hudson, or worse, being towed, to a depot in New Jersey where it is covered with this disgusting plastic substance. Think of the years each ship has spent moored next to other ships of its class, painted, yes, at scheduled times, by a crew of painters whose task it is to paint these ships eternally, finished with one and on to the next and back to the first again five years later. Watchmen watching the ships, year in and year out, no doubt knocking off a little copper pipe here and there—"

"The ships were being stockpiled against a possible new national emergency," I said. "What on earth is wrong with that?"

"I was a messman on the *Saratoga*," he said, "when I was sixteen. I lied about my age."

"But what are your intentions?"

"I am taking these ships away from them," he said.

"You are stealing forty-seven ships from the government of the United States?"

"There are also the submarines," he said. "Six submarines of the Marlin class."

"But why?"

"Remember that I was, once, in accord with them.

Passionately, if I may say so, in accord with them. I did whatever they wished, without thinking, hated their enemies, participated in their crusades, risked my life. Even though I only carried trays and wiped up tables. I heard the singing of the wounded and witnessed the burial of the dead. I believed. Then, over time, I discovered that they were lying. Consistently. With exemplary skill, in a hundred languages. I decided to take the ships. Perhaps they'll notice." He paused. "Now. Do you wish to accompany me, assist me?"

"More than anything."

"Good." He moved the lever of the bridge telegraph to Full Ahead.

Now that I am older I am pleased to remember. Those violent nights. When having laid theorbo aside I came to your bed. You, having laid phonograph aside, lay there. Awaiting. I, having laid aside all cares and other business, approached. Softly so as not to afright the sour censorious authorities. You, undulating restlessly under the dun coverlet. Under the framed, signed and numbered silverprint. I, having laid aside all frets and perturbations, approached.

Prior to this, the meal. Sometimes the meal was taken in, sometimes out. If in, I sliced the onions and tossed them into the pot, or you sliced the chanterelles and tossed them into the pot. The gray glazed pot with the black leopardspot meander. What an infinity of leeks, lentils, turnips, green beans we tossed into the pot, over the years. Celery.

Sometimes the meal was taken out. There we sat properly with others in crowded rooms, green-flocked paper on the walls, the tables too close together. Decent quiet servitors in black-and-white approached and with many marks of respect and good will, fed us. Tingle of choice, sometimes we elected the same dish, lamb in pewter sauce on one occasion. Three yellow daffs and a single red tulip in the tall slender vase to your right. My thumb in my martini nudging the olives from the white plastic sword.

Prior to the meal, the Happy Hour. You removed your shoes and sat, daintily, on your feet. I loosened my tie, if

*the day's business had required one, and held out my
hand. You smashed a glass into it, just in time. Fatigued
from your labors at the scriptorium where you illuminated
manuscripts having to do with the waxing/waning
fortunes of International Snow. We snuggled, there on the
couch, there is no other word for it, as God is my witness.
The bed awaiting.*

*I remember the photograph over your bed. How many
mornings has it greeted me banded with the first timorous
light through the blind-slats. A genuine Weegee, car crash
with prostrate forms, long female hair in a pool of blood
shot through booted cop legs. In a rope-molding frame.
Beside me, your form, not yet awake but bare of dull
unnecessary clothing and excellently positioned to be
prowled over. After full light, tickling permitted.*

*Fleet through the woods came I upon that time toward
your bed. A little pouch of mealie-mealie by my side, for
our repast. You, going into the closet, plucked forth a
cobwebbed bottle. On the table in front of the couch, an
artichoke with its salty dip. Hurling myself through the
shabby tattering door toward the couch, like an (arrow
from the bow) (spear from the hand of Achilles), I thanked
my stars for the wisdom of my teachers, Smoky and Billy,
which had enabled me to find a place in the labor market,
to depart in the morning and return at night, bearing in
the one hand a pannier of periwinkles and in the other, a
disc new-minted by the Hot Club of France.*

Your head in my arms.

Wrack

—Cold here in the garden.
—You were complaining about the sun.
—But when it goes behind a cloud—
—Well, you can't have everything.
—The flowers are beautiful.
—Indeed.
—Consoling to have the flowers.
—Half-way consoled already.
—And these Japanese rocks—
—Artfully placed, most artfully.
—You must admit, a great consolation.
—And Social Security.
—A great consolation.
—And philosophy. Furthermore.
—I read a book. Just the other day.
—Sexuality, too.
—They have books about it. I read one.
—We'll to the woods no more. I assume.
—Where there's a will there's a way. That's what
my mother always said.

—I wonder if it's true.

—I think not.

—Well, you're driving me crazy.

—Well you're driving me crazy too. Know what I mean?

—Going to snap one of these days.

—If you were a Japanese master you wouldn't snap. Those guys never snapped. Some of them were ninety.

—Well, you can't have everything.

—Cold, here in the garden.

—Caw caw caw caw.

—You want to sing that song.

—Can't remember how it goes.

—Getting farther and farther away from life.

—How do you feel about that?

—Guilty but less guilty than I should.

—Can you fine-tune that for me?

—Not yet I want to think about it.

—Well, I have to muck out the stable and buff up the silver.

—They trust you with the silver?

—Of course. I have their trust.

—You enjoy their trust.

—Absolutely.

—Well we still haven't decided what color to paint the trucks.

—I said blue.

—Surely not your last word on the subject.

—I have some swatches. If you'd care to take a gander.

—Not now. This sun is blistering.

—New skin. You're going to complain?

—Thank the Lord for all small favors.

—The kid ever come to see you?

—Did for a while. Then stopped.

—How does that make you feel?

—Oh, I don't blame him.

—Well, you can't have everything.

—That's true. What's the time?

—Looks to be about one.

—Where's your watch?

—Hocked it.

—What'd you get?

—Twelve-fifty.

—God, aren't these flowers beautiful!

—Only three of them. But each remarkable, of its kind.

—What are they?

—Some kind of Japanese dealies I don't know.

—Lazing in the garden. This is really most luxurious.

—Listening to the radio. "Elmer's Tune."

—I don't like it when they let girls talk on the radio.

—Never used to have them. Now they're everywhere.

—You can't really say too much. These days.

—Doesn't that make you nervous? Girls talking on the radio?

—I liked H. V. Kaltenborn. He's long gone.

—What'd you do yesterday?

—Took a walk. In the wild trees.

—They spend a lot of time worrying about where to park their cars. Glad I don't have one.

—Haven't eaten anything except some rice, this morning. Cooked it with chicken broth.

—This place is cold, no getting around it.

—Forgot to buy soap, forgot to buy coffee—

—All right. The hollowed-out book containing the single Swedish municipal bond in the amount of fifty thousand Swedish crowns is not yours. We've established that. Let's go on.

—It was never mine. Or it might have been mine,

once. Perhaps it belonged to my former wife. I said I wasn't sure. She was fond of hiding things in hollowed-out books.

—We want not the shadow of a doubt. We want to be absolutely certain.

—I appreciate it. She had gray eyes. Gray with a touch of violet.

—Yes. Now, are these your doors?

—Yes. I think so. Are they on spring hinges? Do they swing?

—They swing in either direction. Spring hinges. Wood slats.

—She did things with her eyebrows. Painted them gold. You had the gray eyes with a touch of violet, and the gold eyebrows. Yes, the doors must be mine. I seem to remember her bursting through them. In one of the several rages of a summer's day.

—When?

—It must have been some time ago. Some years. I don't know what they're doing here. It strikes me they were in another house. Not this house. I mean it's kind of cloudy.

—But they're here.

—She sometimes threw something through the doorway before bursting through the doorway herself. Acid, on one occasion.

—But the doors are here. They're yours.

—Yes. They seem to be. I mean, I'm not arguing with you. On the other hand, they're not something I want to remember, particularly. They have sort of an unpleasant aura around them, for some reason. I would have avoided them, left to myself.

—I don't want to distress you. Unnecessarily.

—I know, I know, I know. I'm not blaming you, but it just seems to me that you could have let it go. The doors. I'm sure you didn't mean anything by it, but still—

—I didn't mean anything by it. Well, let's leave the doors, then, and go on to the dish.

—Plate.

—Let's go on to the plate, then.

—Plate, dish, I don't care, it's something of an imposition, you must admit, to have to think about it. Normally I wouldn't think about it.

—It has your name on the back. Engraved on the back.

—Where? Show me.

—Your name. Right there. And the date, 1962.

—I don't want to look. I'll take your word for it. That was twenty years ago. My God. She read R. D. Laing. Aloud, at dinner. Every night. Interrupted only by the telephone. When she answered the telephone, her voice became animated. Charming and animated. Gaiety. Vivacity. Laughter. In contrast to her reading of R. D. Laing. Which could only be described as punitive. O.K., so it's mine. My plate.

—It's a dish. A bonbon dish.

—You mean to say that you think that *I* would own a bonbon dish? A sterling-silver or whatever it is bonbon dish? You're mad.

—The doors were yours. Why not the dish?

—A *bonbon* dish?

—Perhaps she craved bonbons?

—No no no no no. Not so. Sourballs, perhaps.

—Let's move on to the shoe, now. I don't have that much time.

—The shoe is definitely not mine.

—Not yours.

—It's a woman's shoe. It's too small for me. My foot, this foot here, would never in the world fit into that shoe.

—I am not suggesting that the shoe is yours in the sense that you wear or would wear such a shoe. It's obviously a woman's shoe.

—The shoe is in no sense a thing of mine. Although found I admit among my things.

—It's here. An old-fashioned shoe. Eleven buttons.

—There was a vogue for that kind of shoe, some time back, among the young people. It might have belonged to a young person. I sometimes saw young persons.

—With what in mind?

—I fondled them, if they were fondleable.

—Within the limits of the law, of course.

—Certainly. "Young person" is an elastic term. You think I'm going to mess with jailbait?

—Of course not. Never occurred to me. The shoe has something of the pathetic about it. A wronged quality. Do you think it possible that the shoe may be in some way a *cri de coeur?*

—Not a chance.

—You were wrong about the dish.

—I've never heard a *cri de coeur.*

—You've never heard a *cri de coeur?*

—Perhaps once. When Shirley was with us?

—Who was Shirley?

—The maid. She was studying eschatology. Maiding parttime. She left us for a better post. Perfectly ordinary departure.

—Did she perhaps wear shoes of this type?

—No. Nor was she given to the *cri de coeur.* Except, perhaps, once. Death of her flying fish. A cry wrenched from her bosom. Rather like a winged phallus it was, she kept it in a washtub in the basement. One day it was discovered belly-up. She screamed. Then, insisted it be given the Last Rites, buried in a fish cemetery, holy water sprinkled this way and that—

—You fatigue me. Now, about the hundred-pound sack of saccharin.

—Mine. Indubitably mine. I'm forbidden to use sugar. I have a condition.

—I'm delighted to hear it. Not that you have a condition but that the sack is, without doubt, yours.

—Mine. Yes.

—I can't tell you how pleased I am. The inquiry moves. Progress is made. Results are obtained.

—What are you writing there, in your notes?

—That the sack is, beyond a doubt, yours.

—I think it's mine.

—What do you mean, *think?* You stated . . . Is it yours or isn't it?

—I think it's mine. It seems to be.

—Seems!

—I just remembered, I put sugar in my coffee. At breakfast.

—Are you sure it wasn't saccharin?

—White powder of some kind . . .

—There is a difference in texture . . .

—No, I remember, it was definitely sugar. Granulated. So the sack of saccharin is definitely not mine.

—Nothing is yours.

—Some things are mine, but the sack is not mine, the shoe is not mine, the bonbon dish is not mine, and the doors are not mine.

—You admitted the doors.

—Not wholeheartedly.

—You said, I have it right here, written down, "Yes, they must be mine."

—Sometimes we hugged. Lengthily. Heart to heart, the one trying to pull the other into the up-right other . . .

—I have it right here. Written down. "Yes, they must be mine."

—I withdraw that.

—You can't withdraw it. I've written it down.

—Nevertheless I withdraw it. It's inadmissible. It was coerced.

—You feel coerced?

—All that business about "dish" rather than "plate"—

—That was a point of fact, it was, in fact, a dish.

—You have a hectoring tone. I don't like to be hectored. You came here with something in mind. You had made an a priori decision.

—That's a little ridiculous when you consider that I have, personally, nothing to gain. Either way. Whichever way it goes.

—Promotion, advancement . . .

—We don't operate that way. That has nothing to do with it. I don't want to discuss this any further. Let's go on to the dressing gown. Is the dressing gown yours?

—Maybe.

—Yes or no?

—My business. Leave it at "maybe."

—I am entitled to a good, solid, answer. Is the dressing gown yours?

—Maybe.

—Please.

—Maybe maybe maybe maybe.

—You exhaust me. In this context, the word "maybe" is unacceptable.

—A perfectly possible answer. People use it every day.

—Unacceptable. What happened to her?

—She made a lot of money. Opened a Palais de Glace, or skating rink. Read R. D. Laing to the skaters over the PA system meanwhile supplementing her income by lecturing over the country as a spokesperson for the unborn.

—The gold eyebrows, still?

—The gold eyebrows and the gray-with-violet eyes. On television, very often.

—In the beginning, you don't know.

—That's true.

—Just one more thing: The two mattresses surrounding the single slice of salami. Are they yours?

—I get hungry. In the night.

—The struggle is admirable. Useless, but admirable. Your struggle.

—Cold, here in the garden.

—You're too old, that's all it is, think nothing of it. Don't give it a thought.

—I haven't agreed to that. Did I agree to that?

—No, I must say you resisted. Admirably, resisted.

—I did resist. Would you allow "valiantly"?

—No no no no. Come come come.

—"Wholeheartedly"?

—Yes, okay, what do I care?

—*Wholeheartedly,* then.

—Yes.

—*Wholeheartedly.*

—We still haven't decided what color to paint the trucks.

—Yes. How about blue?

On our street, fourteen garbage cans are now missing. The garbage cans from One Seventeen and One Nineteen disappeared last night. This is not a serious matter, but on the other hand we can't sit up all night watching over our garbage cans. It is probably best described as an annoyance. One Twelve, One Twenty-two and One Thirty-one have bought new plastic garbage cans at Barney's Hardware to replace those missing. We are thus down eleven garbage cans, net. Many people are using large dark plastic garbage bags. The new construction at the hospital at the end of the block has displaced a number of rats. Rats are not much bothered by plastic garbage bags. In fact, if I were ordered to imagine what might most profitably be invented by a committee of rats, it would be the plastic garbage bag. The rats run up and down our street all night long.

If I were ordered to imagine who is stealing our garbage cans, I could not. I very much doubt that my wife is doing it. Some of the garbage cans on our street are battered metal, others are heavy green plastic. Heavy green plastic or heavy black plastic predominates. Some of the garbage cans have the numbers of the houses they belong to painted on their sides or lids, with white paint. Usually by someone with only the crudest sense of the art of lettering. One Nineteen, which has among its tenants a gifted commercial artist, is an exception. No one excessively famous lives on our street, to my knowledge, therefore the morbid attention that the garbage of the famous sometimes attracts would not be a factor. The

Precinct says that no other street within the precinct has reported similar problems.

If my wife is stealing the garbage cans, in the night, while I am drunk and asleep, what is she doing with them? They are not in the cellar, I've looked (although I don't like going down to the cellar, even to replace a blown fuse, because of the rats). My wife has a yellow Pontiac convertible. No one has these anymore but I can imagine her lifting garbage cans into the back seat of the yellow Pontiac convertible, at two o'clock in the morning, when I am dreaming of being on stage, dreaming of having to perform a drum concerto with only one drumstick . . .

On our street, twenty-one garbage cans are now missing. New infamies have been announced by One Thirty-one through One Forty-three—seven in a row, and on the same side of the street. Also, depredations at One Sixteen and One Sixty-four. We have put out dozens of cans of D-Con but the rats ignore them. Why should they go for the D-Con when they can have the remnants of Ellen Busse's Boeuf Rossini, for which she is known for six blocks in every direction? We eat well, on this street, there's no denying it. Except for the nursing students at One Fifty-eight, and why should they eat well, they're students, are they not? My wife cooks soft-shell crabs, in season, breaded, dusted with tasty cayenne, deep-fried. Barney's Hardware has run out of garbage cans and will not get another shipment until July. Any new garbage cans will have to be purchased at Budget Hardware, far, far away on Second Street.

Petulia, at Custom Care Cleaners, asks why my wife has been acting so peculiar lately. "Peculiar?" I say. "In what way do you mean?" Dr. Maugham, who lives at One Forty-four where he also has his office, has formed a committee. Mr. Wilkens, from One Nineteen, Pally Wimber, from One Twenty-nine, and my wife are on the committee. The committee meets at night, while I sleep,

*dreaming, my turn in the batting order has come up and I
stand at the plate, batless . . .*

There are sixty-two houses on our street, four-story
brownstones for the most part. Fifty-two garbage cans are
now missing. Rats riding upon the backs of other rats
gallop up and down our street, at night. The committee is
unable to decide whether to call itself the Can Committee
or the Rat Committee. The City has sent an inspector who
stood marveling, at midnight, at the activity on our street.
He is filing a report. He urges that the remaining garbage
cans be filled with large stones. My wife has appointed me
a subcommittee of the larger committee with the task of
finding large stones. Is there a peculiar look on her face as
she makes the appointment? Dr. Maugham has bought a
shotgun, a twelve-gauge over-and-under. Mr. Wilkins
has bought a Chase bow and two dozen hunting arrows. I
have bought a flute and an instruction book.

If I were ordered to imagine who is stealing our
garbage cans, the Louis Escher family might spring to
mind, not as culprits but as proximate cause. The Louis
Escher family has a large income and a small apartment,
in One Twenty-one. The Louis Escher family is given to
acquiring things, and given the size of the Louis Escher
apartment, must dispose of old things in order to
accommodate new things. Sometimes the old things
disposed of by the Louis Escher family are scarcely two
weeks old. Therefore, the garbage at One Twenty-one is
closely followed in the neighborhood, in the sense that the
sales and bargains listed in the newspapers are closely
followed. The committee, which feels that the garbage of
the Louis Escher family may be misrepresenting the
neighborhood to the criminal community, made a partial
list of the items disposed of by the Louis Escher family
during the week of August eighth: one mortar & pestle,
majolica ware; one English cream maker (cream is made
by mixing unsalted sweet butter and milk); one set green
earthenware geranium leaf plates; one fruit ripener

designed by scientists at the University of California,
plexiglass; one nylon umbrella tent with aluminum poles;
one combination fountain pen and clock with LED
readout; one mini hole-puncher-and-confetti-maker; one
pistol-grip spring-loaded flyswatter; one cast-iron tortilla
press; one ivory bangle with elephant-hair accent; and
much, much more. But while I do not doubt that the
excesses of the Louis Escher family are misrepresenting the
neighborhood to the criminal community, I cannot bring
myself to support even a resolution of censure, since the
excesses of the Louis Escher family have given us much to
talk about and not a few sets of green earthenware
geranium leaf plates over the years.

I reported to my wife that large stones were hard to
come by in the city. "Stones," she said. "Large stones." I
purchased two hundred pounds of Sakrete at Barney's
Hardware, to make stones with. One need only add water
and stir, and you have made a stone as heavy and brutish
as a stone made by God himself. I am temporarily busy, in
the basement, shaping Sakrete to resemble this, that and
the other, but mostly stones—a good-looking stone is not
the easiest of achievements. Ritchie Beck, the little boy
from One Ten who is always alone on the sidewalk during
the day, smiling at strangers, helps me. I once bought him
a copy of Mechanix Illustrated, which I myself read
avidly as a boy. Harold, who owns Custom Care Cleaners
and also owns a Cessna, has offered to fly over our street
at night and drop bombs made of lethal dry-cleaning fluid
on the rats. There is a channel down the Hudson he can
take (so long as he stays under eleven hundred feet), a
quick left turn, the bombing run, then a dash back up the
Hudson. They will pull his ticket if he's caught, he says,
but at that hour of the night . . . I show my wife the new
stones. "I don't like them," she says. "They don't look like
real stones." She is not wrong, they look, in fact, like
badly-thrown pots, as if they had been done by a potter
with no thumbs. The committee, which has named itself the

*Special Provisional Unnecessary Rat Team (SPURT),
has acquired armbands and white steel helmets and is
discussing a secret grip by which its members will identify
themselves to each other.*

*There are now no garbage cans on our street—no
garbage cans left to steal. A committee of rats has joined
with the Special Provisional committee in order to deal
with the situation, which, the rats have made known, is
attracting unwelcome rat elements from other areas of the
city. Members of the two committees exchange secret grips.
My wife drives groups of rats here and there in her yellow
Pontiac convertible, attending important meetings. The
crisis, she says, will be a long one. She has never been
happier.*

The Palace at Four A.M.

My father's kingdom was and is, all authorities agree, large. To walk border to border east-west, the traveler must budget no less than seventeen days. Its name is Ho, the Confucian term for harmony. Confucianism was an interest of the first ruler (a strange taste in our part of the world), and when he'd cleared his expanse of field and forest of his enemies, two centuries ago, he indulged himself in an *hommage* to the great Chinese thinker, much to the merriment of some of our staider neighbors, whose domains were proper Luftlunds and Dolphinlunds. We have an economy based upon truffles, in which our forests are spectacularly rich, and electricity, which we were exporting when other countries still read by kerosene lamp. Our army is the best in the region, every man a colonel—the subtle secret of my father's rule, if the truth be known. In this land every priest

is a bishop, every ambulance-chaser a robed
justice, every peasant a corporation and every
street-corner shouter Kant himself. My
father's genius was to promote his subjects,
male and female, across the board, ceaselessly;
the people of Ho warm themselves forever in
the sun of Achievement. I was the only man
in the kingdom who thought himself a
donkey.

—FROM THE *Autobiography*

I am writing to you, Hannahbella, from a distant
country. I daresay you remember it well. The King
encloses the opening pages of his autobiography. He
is most curious as to what your response to them will
be. He has labored mightily over their composition,
working without food, without sleep, for many days
and nights.

The King has not been, in these months, in the
best of spirits. He has read your article and declares
himself to be very much impressed by it. He begs
you, prior to publication in this country, to do him
the great favor of changing the phrase "two disinterested and impartial arbiters" on page thirty-one
to "malign elements under the ideological sway of
still more malign elements." Otherwise, he is delighted. He asks me to tell you that your touch is as
adroit as ever.

Early in the autobiography (as you see) we en-
counter the words: "My mother the Queen made a
mirror pie, a splendid thing the size of a poker table
. . ." The King wishes to know if poker tables are in
use in faraway lands, and whether the reader in such
places would comprehend the dimensions of the pie.
He continues: ". . . in which reflections from the
kitchen chandelier exploded when the crew rolled it
from the oven. We were kneeling side-by-side, peer-

ing into the depths of a new-made mirror pie, when my mother said to me, or rather her celestial image said to my dark, heavy-haired one, 'Get out. I cannot bear to look upon your donkey face again.'"

The King wishes to know, Hannahbella, whether this passage seems to you tainted by self-pity, or is, rather, suitably dispassionate.

He walks up and down the small room next to his bedchamber, singing your praises. The decree having to do with your banishment will be rescinded, he says, the moment you agree to change the phrase "two disinterested and impartial arbiters" to "malign elements," etc. This I urge you to do with all speed.

The King has not been at his best. Peace, he says, is an unnatural condition. The country is prosperous, yes, and he understands that the people value peace, that they prefer to spin out their destinies in placid, undisturbed fashion. But *his* destiny, he says, is to alter the map of the world. He is considering several new wars, small ones, he says, small but interesting, complex, dicey, even. He would very much like to consult with you about them. He asks you to change, on page forty-four of your article, the phrase "egregious usurpations" to "symbols of benign transformation." Please initial the change on the proofs, so that historians will not accuse us of bowdlerization.

Your attention is called to the passage in the pages I send which runs as follows: "I walked out of the castle at dusk, not even the joy of a new sunrise to console me, my shaving kit with its dozen razors (although I shaved a dozen times a day, the head was still a donkey's) banging against the Walther .22 in my rucksack. After a time I was suddenly quite tired. I lay down under a hedge by the side of the road. One of the bushes above me had a shred of black cloth tied to it, a sign, in our country, that the place was haunted (but my head's enough to frighten any ghost)." Do you remember that shred of black cloth, Hannahbella? "I ate a slice of my mother's spinach pie and considered my situation. My princeliness would win me an evening, perhaps a fortnight, at this or that noble's castle in the vicinity, but my experience of visiting had taught me that neither royal blood nor novelty of aspect prevailed for long against a host's natural preference for folk with heads much like his own. Should I en-zoo myself? Volunteer for a traveling circus? Attempt the stage? The question was most vexing.

"I had not wiped the last crumbs of the spinach pie from my whiskers when something lay down beside me, under the hedge.

"'What's this?' I said.

"'Soft,' said the new arrival, 'don't be afraid, I am a bogle, let me abide here for the night, your back is warm and that's a mercy.'

"'What's a bogle?' I asked, immediately fetched, for the creature was small, not at all frightening to look upon and clad in female flesh, something I do not hold in low esteem.

"'A bogle,' said the tiny one, with precision, 'is not a black dog.'

"Well, I thought, now I know.

"'A bogle,' she continued, 'is not a boggart.'

"'Delighted to hear it,' I said.

"'Don't you ever *shave?*' she asked. 'And why have you that huge hideous head on you, that could be mistaken for the head of an ass, could I see better so as to think better?'

"'You may lie elsewhere,' I said, 'if my face discountenances you.'

"'I am fatigued,' she said, 'go to sleep, we'll discuss it in the morning, move a bit so that your back fits better with my front, it will be cold, later, and this place is cursed, so they say, and I hear that the Prince has been driven from the palace, God knows what that's all about but it promises no good for us plain folk, police, probably, running all over the fens with their identity checks and making you blow up their great balloons with your breath—'

"She was confusing, I thought, several issues, but my God! she was warm and shapely. Yet I deemed her a strange piece of goods, and made the mistake of saying so.

"'Sir,' she answered, 'I would not venture upon what's strange and what's not strange, if I were you,' and went on to say that if I did not abstain from further impertinence she would commit sewerpipe. She dropped off to sleep then, and I lay back upon the ground. Not a child, I could tell, rather a tiny woman. A bogle."

The King wishes you to know, Hannahbella, that he finds this passage singularly moving and that he cannot read it without being forced to take snuff, violently. Similarly the next:

"What, precisely, is a donkey? As you may imagine, I have researched the question. My *Larousse* was most delicate, as if the editors thought the matter blushful, but yielded two observations of interest: that donkeys came originally from Africa, and that they, or we, are 'the result of much crossing.' This urges that the parties to the birth must be ill-matched, and in the case of my royal parents, 'twas thunderously true. The din of their calamitous conversations reached every quarter of the palace, at every season of the year. My mother named me Duncan (var. of Dunkey, clearly) and went into spasms of shrinking whenever, youthfully, I'd offer a cheek for a kiss. My father, in contrast, could sometimes bring himself to scratch my head between the long, weedlike ears, but only, I suspect, by means of a mental shift, as if he were addressing one of his hunting dogs, the which, incidentally, remained firmly ambivalent about me even after long acquaintance.

"I explained a part of this to Hannahbella, for that was the bogle's name, suppressing chiefly the fact that I was a prince. She in turn gave the following account of herself. She was indeed a bogle, a semi-spirit generally thought to be of bad character. This was a libel, she said, as her own sterling qualities would quickly persuade me. She was, she said, of the utmost perfection in the female line, and there was not a woman within the borders of the kingdom so beautiful as herself, she'd been told it a thousand times. It was true, she went on, that she was not of a standard size, could in fact be called small, if not minuscule, but those who objected to this were louts and fools and might usefully be stewed in lead, for the entertainment of the countryside. In the matter of rank and precedence, the meanest bogle outweighed the greatest king, although the kings of this earth, she conceded, would never acknowledge this but in their dotty solipsism conducted themselves as if bogles did not even exist. And would I like to see her all unclothed so that I might glean some rude idea as to the true nature of the sublime?

"Well, I wouldn't have minded a bit. She was wonderfully crafted, that was evident, and held in addition the fascination surrounding any perfect miniature. But I said, 'No, thank you. Perhaps another day, it's a bit chill this morning.'

"'Just the breasts then,' she said, 'they're wondrous pretty,' and before I could protest further she'd whipped off her mannikin's tiny shirt. I buttoned her up again meanwhile bestowing buckets of extravagant praise. 'Yes,' she said in agreement, 'that's how I am all over, wonderful.'"

The King cannot reread this section, Hannah-bella, without being reduced to tears. The world is a wilderness, he says, civilization a folly we entertain in concert with others. He himself, at his age, is beyond surprise, yet yearns for it. He longs for the conversations he formerly had with you, in the deepest hours of the night, he in his plain ermine robe, you simply dressed as always in a small scarlet cassock, most becoming, a modest supper of chicken, fruit and wine on the sideboard, only the pair of you awake in the whole palace, at four o'clock in the morning. The tax evasion case against you has been dropped. It was, he says, a hasty and ill-considered undertaking, even spiteful. He is sorry.

The King wonders whether the following paragraphs from his autobiography accord with your own recollections: "She then began, as we walked down the road together (an owl pretending to be absent standing on a tree limb to our left, a little stream snapping and growling to our right), explaining to me that my father's administration of the realm left much to be desired, from the bogle point of view, particularly his mad insistence on filling the forests with heavy-footed truffle hounds. Standing, she came to just a hand above my waist; her hair was brown, with bits of gold in it; her quite womanly hips were encased in rust-colored trousers. 'Duncan,' she said, stabbing me in the calf with her sharp nails, 'do you know what that man has done? Nothing else but ruin, absolutely ruin, the whole of the Gatter Fen with a great roaring electric plant that makes a thing that who in the world could have a use for I don't know. I think they're called volts. Two square miles of first-class fen paved over. We bogles are being squeezed to our knees.' I had a sudden urge to kiss her, she looked so angry, but did nothing, my history in this regard being, as I have said, infelicitous.

"'Duncan, *you're not listening!'* Hannahbella was naming the chief interesting things about bogles, which included the fact that in the main they had nothing to do with humans, or nonsemispirits; that although she might seem small to me she was tall, for a bogle, queenly, in fact; that there was a type of blood seas superior to royal blood, and that it was bogle blood; that bogles had no magical powers whatsoever, despite what was said of them; that bogles were the very best lovers in the whole world, no matter what class of thing, animal, vegetable, or insect, might be under discussion; that it was not true that bogles knocked bowls of mush from the tables of the deserving poor and caused farmers' cows to become pregnant with big fishes, out of pure mischief; that female bogles were the most satisfactory sexual partners of any kind of thing that could ever be imagined and were especially keen for large overgrown things with ass's ears, for example; and that there was a something in the road ahead of us to which it might, perhaps, be prudent to pay heed.

"She was right. One hundred yards ahead of us, planted squarely athwart the road, was an army."

The King, Hannahbella, regrets having said of you, in the journal *Vu,* that you have two brains and no heart. He had thought he was talking not-for-attribution, but as you know, all reporters are scoundrels and not to be trusted. He asks you to note that *Vu* has suspended publication and to recall that it was never read by anyone but serving maids and the most insignificant members of the minor clergy. He is prepared to give you a medal, if you return, any medal you like—you will remember that our medals are the most gorgeous going. On page seventy-five of your article, he requires you, most humbly, to change "monstrous over-reaching fueled by an insatiable if still childish ego" to any kinder construction of your choosing.

The King's autobiography, in chapters already written but which I do not enclose, goes on to recount how you and he together, by means of a clever stratagem of your devising, vanquished the army barring your path on that day long, long ago; how the two of you journeyed together for many weeks and found that your souls were, in essence, the same soul; the shrewd means you employed to place him in power, against the armed opposition of the Party of the Lily, on the death of his father; and the many subsequent campaigns which you endured together, mounted on a single horse, your armor banging against his armor. The King's autobiography, Hannahbella, will run to many volumes, but he cannot bring himself to write the end of the story without you.

The King feels that your falling-out, over the matter of the refugees from Brise, was the result of a miscalculation on his part. He could not have known, he says, that they had bogle blood (although he admits that the fact of their small stature should have told him something). Exchanging the refugees from Brise for the twenty-three Bishops of Ho captured during the affair was, he says in hindsight, a serious error; more bishops can always be created. He makes the point that you did not tell him that the refugees from Brise had bogle blood but instead expected him to know it. Your outrage was, he thinks, a pretext. He at once forgives you and begs your forgiveness. The Chair of Military Philosophy at the university is yours, if you want it. You loved him, he says, he is convinced of it, he still cannot believe it, he exists in a condition of doubt. You are both old; you are both forty. The palace at four A.M. is silent. Come back, Hannahbella, and speak to him.

I am, at the moment, seated. On a stump in the forest,
listening. Ireland and Scotland are remote, Wales is not
near. I will rise, soon, to hold the ladder for you.

Tombs are scattered through the tall, white beanwoods.
They are made of perfectly ordinary gray stone. Chan-
deliers, at night, scatter light over the tombs, little houses
in which I sleep with the already-beautiful, and they with
me. The already-beautiful saunter through the forest
carrying plump red hams, already cooked. The already-
beautiful do not, as a rule, run.

Holding the ladder I watch you glue additional
chandeliers to appropriate limbs. You are tiring, you have
worked very hard. Iced beanwater will refresh you, and
these wallets made of ham. I have set bronze statues of
alert, crouching Indian boys around the periphery of the
forest, for ornamentation. For ornamentation. Each alert,
crouching Indian boy is accompanied by a large, bronze,
wolf-like dog, finely polished.

I have been meaning to speak to you. I have many
pages of notes, instructions, quarrels. On weighty matters
I will speak without notes, freely and passionately, as if
inspired, at night, in a rage, slapping myself, great
tremendous slaps to the brow which will fell me to the
earth. The already-beautiful will stand and watch, in a
circle, cradling, each, an animal in mothering arms—
green monkey, meadow mouse, tucotuco.

That one has her hips exposed, for study. I make careful

notes. *You snatch the notebook from my hands. The
pockets of your smock swing heavily with the lights of
chandeliers. Your light-by-light, bean-by-bean career.
I am, at this moment, prepared to dance.
The already-beautiful have, historically, danced. The
music made by my exercise machine is, we agree,
danceable. The women partner themselves with large
bronze hares, which have been cast in the attitudes of
dancers. The beans you have glued together are as nothing
to the difficulty of casting hares in the attitudes of dancers,
at night, in the foundry, working the bellows, the sweat,
the glare. The heat. The glare.
Thieves have been invited to dinner, along with the
deans of the chief cathedrals. The thieves will rest upon
the bosoms of the deans, at night, after dinner, after
coffee, among the beanwoods. The thieves will confess to
the deans, and the deans to the thieves. Soft benedictions
will ensue.
England is far away, and France is but a rumor.
Pillows are placed in the tombs, potholders, dustcloths. I
am privileged, privileged, to be able to hold your ladder.
Tirelessly you glue. The forest will soon exist on some
maps, tribute to the quickness of the world's cartographers.
This life is better than any I have lived, previously.
Beautiful hips bloom and part. Your sudden movement
toward red kidney beans has proved, in the event,
masterly. Everywhere we see the already-beautiful wearing
stomachers, tiaras of red kidney beans, polished to the
fierceness of carnelians. No ham hash does not contain
two red kidney beans, polished to the fierceness of
carnelians.
Spain is distant, Portugal wrapped in an impenetrable
haze. These noble beans, glued by you, are mine.
Thousand-pound sacks are off-loaded at the quai, against
our future needs. The deans are willing workers, the*

thieves, straw bosses of extraordinary tact. Your weather reports have been splendid: the fall of figs you predicted did in fact occur. I am, at the moment, feeling very jolly. Hey hey, I say. It is remarkable how well human affairs can be managed, with care.

Overnight to
Many Distant Cities

A group of Chinese in brown jackets preceded us through the halls of Versailles. They were middle-aged men, weighty, obviously important, perhaps thirty of them. At the entrance to each room a guard stopped us, held us back until the Chinese had finished inspecting it. A fleet of black government Citroëns had brought them, they were much at ease with Versailles and with each other, it was clear that they were being rewarded for many years of good behavior.

Asked her opinion of Versailles, my daughter said she thought it was overdecorated.

Well, yes.

Again in Paris, years earlier, without Anna, we had a hotel room opening on a courtyard, and late at night through an open window heard a woman expressing intense and rising pleasure. We blushed and fell upon each other.

Right now sunny skies in mid-Manhattan, the temperature is forty-two degrees.

In Stockholm we ate reindeer steak and I told the Prime Minister . . . That the price of booze was too high. Twenty dollars for a bottle of J & B! He (Olof Palme) agreed, most politely, and said that they financed the army that way. The conference we were attending was held at a workers' vacation center somewhat outside the city. Shamelessly, I asked for a double bed, there were none, we pushed two single beds together. An Israeli journalist sat on the two single beds drinking our costly whiskey and explaining the devilish policies of the Likud. Then it was time to go play with the Africans. A poet who had been for a time a Minister of Culture explained why he had burned a grand piano on the lawn in front of the Ministry. "The piano," he said, "is not the national instrument of Uganda."

A boat ride through the scattered islands. A Warsaw Pact novelist asked me to carry a package of paper to New York for him.

Woman is silent for two days in San Francisco. And walked through the streets with her arms raised high touching the leaves of the trees.

"But you're *married!*"

"But that's *not my fault!*"

Tearing into cold crab at Scoma's we saw Chill Wills at another table, doing the same thing. We waved to him.

In Taegu the air was full of the noise of helicopters. The helicopter landed on a pad, General A jumped out and walked with a firm, manly stride to the spot where General B waited—generals visiting each other. They shook hands, the honor guard with its blue scarves and chromed rifles popped to, the band played, pictures were taken. General A followed by

General B walked smartly around the rigid honor guard and then the two generals marched off to the General's Mess, to have a drink.

There are eight hundred and sixty-one generals now on active service. There are four hundred and twenty-six brigadier generals, three hundred and twenty-four major generals, eighty-seven lieutenant generals, and twenty-four full generals. The funniest thing in the world is a general trying on a nickname. Sometimes they don't stick. "Howlin' Mad," "Old Hickory," "Old Blood and Guts," and "Buck" have already been taken. "Old Lacy" is not a good choice.

If you are a general in the field you will live in a general's van, which is a kind of motor home for generals. I once saw a drunk two-star general, in a general's van, seize hold of a visiting actress—it was Marilyn Monroe—and seat her on his lap, shrieking all the while "R.H.I.P.!" or, Rank Has Its Privileges.

Enough of generals.

Thirty per cent chance of rain this afternoon, high in the mid-fifties.

In London I met a man who was not in love. Beautiful shoes, black as black marble, and a fine suit. We went to the theatre together, matter of a few pounds, he knew which plays were the best plays, on several occasions he brought his mother. "An American," he said to his mother, "an American I met." "Met an American during the war," she said to me, "didn't like him." This was reasonably standard, next she would tell me that we had no culture. Her son was hungry, starving, mad in fact, sucking the cuff buttons of his fine suit, choking on the cuff buttons of his fine suit, left and right sleeves jammed into his mouth—he was not in love, he said, "again not in love, not in love again." I put him out of his misery

with a good book, Rilke, as I remember, and re-
solved never to find myself in a situation as dire as
his.

In San Antonio we walked by the little river. And
ended up in Helen's Bar, where John found a pool
player who was, like John, an ex-Marine. How these
ex-Marines love each other! It is a flat scandal. The
Congress should do something about it. The IRS
should do something about it. You and I talked to
each other while John talked to his Parris Island
friend, and that wasn't too bad, wasn't too bad. We
discussed twenty-four novels of normative adultery.
"Can't *have* no adultery without adults," I said, and
you agreed that this was true. We thought about it,
our hands on each other's knees, under the table.

In the car on the way back from San Antonio the
ladies talked about the rump of a noted poet. "Too
big," they said, "too big too big too big." "Can you
imagine going to bed with him?" they said, and then
all said "No no no no no," and laughed and laughed
and laughed and laughed and laughed.

I offered to get out and run alongside the car, if
that would allow them to converse more freely.

In Copenhagen I went shopping with two Hungarians. I
had thought they merely wanted to buy presents for
their wives. They bought leather gloves, chess sets,
frozen fish, baby food, lawnmowers, air condi-
tioners, kayaks. . . . We were six hours in the department store.

"This will teach you," they said, "never to go shopping with Hungarians."

Again in Paris, the hotel was the Montalembert . . .
Anna jumped on the bed and sliced her hand open
on an open watercolor tin, blood everywhere, the
concierge assuring us that "In the war, I saw much
worse things."

Well, yes.

But we couldn't stop the bleeding, in the cab to the American Hospital the driver kept looking over his shoulder to make sure that we weren't bleeding on his seat covers, handfuls of bloody paper towels in my right and left hands . . .

On another evening, as we were on our way to dinner, I kicked the kid with carefully calibrated force as we were crossing the Pont Mirabeau, she had been pissy all day, driving us crazy, her character improved instantly, wonderfully, this is a tactic that can be used exactly once.

In Mexico City we lay with the gorgeous daughter of the American ambassador by a clear, cold mountain stream. Well, that was the plan, it didn't work out that way. We were around sixteen and had run away from home, in the great tradition, hitched various long rides with various sinister folk, and there we were in the great city with about two t-shirts to our names. My friend Herman found us jobs in a jukebox factory. Our assignment was to file the slots in American jukeboxes so that they would accept the big, thick Mexican coins. All day long. No gloves.

After about a week of this we were walking one day on the street on which the Hotel Reforma is to be found and there were my father and grandfather, smiling. "The boys have run away," my father had told my grandfather, and my grandfather had said, "Hot damn, let's go get 'em." I have rarely seen two grown men enjoying themselves so much.

Ninety-two this afternoon, the stock market up in heavy trading.

In Berlin everyone stared, and I could not blame them. You were spectacular, your long skirts, your long dark hair. I was upset by the staring, people gazing at happiness and wondering whether to credit it or not, wondering whether it was to be trusted and for how long, and what it meant to them, whether they

were in some way hurt by it, in some way diminished
by it, in some way criticized by it, good God get it out
of my sight—

I correctly identified a Matisse as a Matisse even
though it was an uncharacteristic Matisse, you
thought I was knowledgeable whereas I was only
lucky, we stared at the Schwitters show for one hour
and twenty minutes, and then lunched. Vitello ton-
nato, as I recall.

When Herman was divorced in Boston . . . Carol got
the good barbeque pit. I put it in the Blazer for her.
In the back of the Blazer were cartons of books,
tableware, sheets and towels, plants, and oddly, two
dozen white carnations fresh in their box. I pointed
to the flowers. "Herman," she said, "he never gives
up."

In Barcelona the lights went out. At dinner. Candles
were produced and the shiny langoustines placed
before us. Why do I love Barcelona above most
other cities? Because Barcelona and I share a pas-
sion for walking? I was happy there? You were with
me? We were celebrating my hundredth marriage?
I'll stand on that. Show me a man who has not married a hundred times and I'll show you a wretch who
does not deserve the world.

Lunching with the Holy Ghost I praised the
world, and the Holy Ghost was pleased. "We have
that little problem in Barcelona," He said, "the lights
go out in the middle of dinner." "I've noticed," I
said. "We're working on it," He said, "what a wonderful city, one of our best." "A great town," I
agreed. In an ecstasy of admiration for what is we
ate our simple soup.

Tomorrow, fair and warmer, warmer and fair,
most fair. . . .